God, Make Me White!
The "Black" Girl Prayed

Altagracia Cabrera

Lo dedico con cariño para, Alexis, ~~Alexis~~ Alaase, Autumne y Amiyah.

LACUHE
Ediciones

Illustrated by: Erlin Omar Capellán
Proofreaders in Spanish: Miguel Ángel Capellán,
Teresita Brache, Gina and Lic. Oscar López Reyes
Translated by: Dinorah Coronado and Hansel Soriano
Cover and interior design by Yorman Mejías
Printed in United States of America

We are a perfect jewelry case,
full of virtues and defects.

Beauty exists only in
the eyes of those who see it.

I look good, I don't understand
why you see me otherwise.

Table of contents

Dedication

This book is dedicated, especially, to all those who manage to survive this important stage in human development: childhood; apparently a simple stage, yet difficult to overcome. A phase marked with indelible ink, words, gestures, and actions of the surrounding world. These are the true architects of the behavior and character of future citizens.

At the same time, I raise my voice for those who have not been able to avoid the barriers and obstacles raised against them that prevent their advancement and growth. For those who escaped through the shortest route, but not the appropriate one. For those under pressure who thought suicide would free them from the psychological tortures caused by the iniquities of their peers. For those who left their father, mother, siblings, grandparents, friends, and even strangers submerged in pain and impotence. Suicide is a path that entangles more suffering than happy endings. Therefore, it should not be an option to avoid life's difficulties. Life is limited and so are rough times.

I address bullies and oppressors regardless of age: stop, reflect and become aware enough to coexist in peace and friendship with your peers.

To all those lacking the great virtue of sharing the peace chalice: love, understanding and respect of others' right to be different, as our Creator wishes.

Nevertheless, I dedicate this story to all audiences.

Acknowledgements

Thank God, who's given me life.

I thank the memory of my mother who continues to live in me, because she was my best teacher.

To my daughter and my three sons, for their contributions to my life.

To my grandchildren.

To my son–in–law Gregorio, who also put his effort in this endeavor and who has supported me as his mother–in–law.

Thanks, because all of you, in one way or another, have shown unconditional love to me. I love you all.

To my three brothers, who were the engine of my childhood days.

To my friends, colleagues and coworkers, who shared a lot of their time and raised my self–esteem.

Thanks to all my brothers and sisters in Christ, who ask for God's blessing every day.

To all those children: girls, boys and teenagers who at some point in their lives honored me by adopting me as a mother. Especially to my angel Michel, who left this earth before me at a very early age. That little angel will welcome me into heaven, on the day that God takes me away from this Earth. There he will also call me "mom" with his sweet voice, and he will remember how much I loved him, and I thanked him for having chosen me as a mother in his last years of life. That was a true honor for me.

Thanks to Teresita Brache, who was the first to evaluate and approve the content of this book.

Miguel, my number one proofreader.

Thanks to Oscar López Reyes, my teacher.

A special Thank You to my husband, who for more than three decades has been an unconditional partner, always willing to show his love for me and his children. Thank you because you have been able to withstand my defects and to value my virtues. Thanks also, for waking me up with love in the morning, offering me a rich, freshly brewed coffee.

Thank you all for filling my life with love.

God, Make Me White!
The "Black" Girl Prayed

Altagracia Cabrera

Chapter I

Barely standing on thin legs and bony knees, an ordinary girl goes unnoticed from the rest of the world. Accompanied by the urgent silence of the small room, which she shares with her mother; she begins a communion with God filled with passion.

Disappointedly, she assumed that it was time to reveal the childhood faith that fervently lived in her heart.

In an unconscious, almost mechanical manner, the girl gazes with tenderness at the shimmering rays coming from the lamp that sat on the mahogany table, one of the two that her mother kept as a family antique, inherited from her grandmother.

She concentrates her attention on the thin beam of light that was sneaking through the gaps of the old tinplate sheets, which rested on the deteriorated wooden trestle, already struck by the severity of the unstable tropical climate.

Tati goes through her subconscious, submerging herself in the haze of her very special moments. As the afternoon settles, the usual serenity begins to permeate the populous neighborhood of Vietnam leaving those last hours, when daily activity almost completely fades, overwhelmed by the choking of the last of the sizzling midday sun. Only the voice of the neighborhood barker minimally breaks through the barriers of the silence of the restful evening.

Oblivious to all external occurrences, Tati frees herself from a strong internal battle. It is not an easy battle to win, no, no, no, her struggle is against Celestial Monarchs, Powers of authority, against the ghosts that reside in the deepest part of her subconscious. The tender creature cries out to the Supreme Being, the one who created her in her mother's womb, in whom she trusts, the only One who can change what troubles her to her core.

—It's the best time to say this —Tati repeats aloud, (no one will listen, nobody's home). She reaches out from the depths of her heart her most sincere prayer, and pleads: —God, make me white!

No one could have imagined years ago, when Tati was a small and innocent creature,

14

of the inception of this sequence of events that would bring her to this moment.

—God, make me white -the girl pleads again.

At this time, she is possessed and dazed by a soft whirlwind that wraps around her completely, her surroundings start to change as if by magic. The small room she shares with her mother becomes large and welcoming.

There is now a very elegantly made bed with soft and delicate pink linens where a few days ago only a flowery sheet hung over a humble bed. The ceiling had been cleaned so that I well it looked like snow from a Christmas story illustration. The place where Tati rests her knees now is made up of bright, refined marble. In her subconscious, she pictures herself laid out in that warm, cozy space. The clock stops. Her mind leaves her for a while, until she tells herself with a smile on her lips, "To be white, is what I'm asking for", as if responding to a question made by the Almighty. Her strength abandons her, she wants to raise her voice again but the words do not come out of her.

Suddenly, a shiver runs through Tati's small frame from head to toe. The time had elapsed, confirmed by the reverberating voice of the baker, humming the characteristics of the warm bread he is offering for dinner. Oblivious to everything on the outside, with her big eyes still closed, she repeats for the third time:

—God, make me white!

Still in a daze, the girl is flooded with vivid images running through her subconscious like a film strip, projecting memories she thought dead. Well, there they are now, those exact scenes that led to this moment of her life.

Tati feels her skin shrinking, mercilessly tightening around her tissues. Instantly, she visualizes herself in the sixties, in an overpopulated neighborhood of Santo Domingo -the capital of the Dominican Republic— surrounded by the rest of her small world that witnessed a black girl growing up.

The moment flashes right before her eyes of the day her family was welcomed by the famous Los Mina neighborhood. A silent testimony to the enormous territorial

expansion that the capital city was
experiencing, in pursuit of its inevitable
demographic growth. At that time, Tati was
barely two years old. And of course, she
cared less about these things.

In her unconscious race through time and
space, she penetrates through the deep
threshold of her mind and walks between the
two rows of shacks that make up K1 Street.
At that moment she goes to one of the
humblest of the small houses she ever lived
in, right on the edge of the sidewalk. She
does not let the personal grief take over, but
starts to relive the moments in which
everything seemed rosy. The period in which
playing and running around with the
butterflies meant the most important part of
her days.

With the best family in the known
Universe Tati was enjoying the love of her
mother, who had given her the nickname
Tati.

The selfless small woman with cinnamon
skin was the mother that any child would
want to have. The little girl grew up extremely
happy, along with the rest of the family that
lived with them.

The second half of the 20th century was just starting, where the great ideas of Baise Pascal and his "Pascalina" had not been exploited yet; nor the great contribution of Scottish John Logie Baird for the broadcast of television signals —which in the future would constitute a great emporium of entertainment. The essence of family was very crucial and the absence of the most brilliant technologies were reflected around them. Eight was the minimum in the average of members per family at the time. They were only five in total, below the normal family average.

Tati traveled in time remembering her mother's story when at dawn —on the second day of a February like any other— she had first seen the light of the day weighing only two and a half pounds. The mother laughed when she said that she did not know how to hold that fragile little body.

—Imagine! All my children were born weighing over eight pounds. One of them weighed ten. I thought that wherever I touched you I could fracture your tiny bones —said the mother.
—I was so happy yet afraid to hurt her. When she arrived in my life my family was finally complete. What else could I ask for? I

did not expect to have any more children and even so, God rewarded me with one more child. On my way to fifty, my reproductive cycle had shut down. Then I had a pregnancy that lasted for what seemed like ten months — she said in full laughter.

—That was my biggest belly, much, much bigger than the previous ones, and in the end I gave birth to a little doll that only weighed two and a half pounds, the irony of life...

Her three brothers made her feel like a princess in her castle. The eldest, a bug—eyed teenager with a thick unibrow, was chosen by fate to endure hard work, marked on his look and shoulders.

The three titans were each unique in their treatment of Tati. The second, almost seven years younger, was an absolute leader of robust appearance, and stood out with his long face and upturned nose. He had the look of a saint on the Church altar. In contrast to the other two, the third one devoted his attention among those around him. He was a clever individual, of agile fists, and willing to frighten those who wanted to start trouble.

The mother, through her joy, viewed her children equally. The love and protection that they always gave her was the engine of Tati's existence, even when a fatherly figure was absent. Everything worked so perfectly in the home that the absence of her father no longer mattered, or at least that's what it seemed like.

At the dawn and twilight of each day, happiness played the leading role for each of the family members. Nonetheless, the imminent events that mark the mind and heart of a young one are countless; regardless of gender, age, race or social class.

Chapter II

That unforgettable timeframe when everything seemed beautiful and unfamiliar at the same time, when being a four—year—old child made you reminisce with unmistakable innocence has been engraved in Tati's mind. Back then material things were of little importance. The sphere of household appliances shone even more in their absence, especially in the homes of poor families. In those days, poverty was poverty, and wealth was wealth. Both social classes were clearly marked, being poor was synonymous with having nothing. Lacking anything —above the minimum— was enough to survive.

The scant furnishings of each shack were no more than a bed and a couple of chairs for a group of more than ten people. The humble houses were built with refuse, from materials collected or purchased second or third hand. They were built with enough space between each other, for the land was plentiful while the materials to build were scare. An allegorical name of a historical character would be used to identify and give flair to the neighborhood. Everything was wonderful, despite the roof covered with palm fronds or the rusted tin sheets that served as walls. Five, seven, nine, and even sometimes more than a dozen kids were running around, laughing loudly in every corner, and one or two beds were more than enough to be sent to dreamland each night.

There is Tati now, in front of the nicest house, that of Doña Librada —the one lady in the neighborhood that was better off— waiting for the raspberry ice cream she had requested. As luck would have it, almost every poor neighborhood had that one family that was doing better and had a fridge in the kitchen and a television set in the living room inside their fancy clapboard siding homes.

Tati smiles now, feeling like she still lives there, and has forgetting about the present. Two of her brothers are impatiently waiting around her to have a taste of her raspberry ice cream. Of course, she doesn't want to share it. As she holds it, she feels that her hands are freezing with the cold emanating from the ice cream. The chills lead to another memory that of the portable stove placed in a corner of the courtyard by her mother steaming with boiling water to cook the plantains.

Tati can still hear the strong voice of her mother, saying to her innocent, obedient second son:

—I'm home, son! I came earlier because I have an errand — she put on her nylon stockings with extreme care, the ones she only used in special occasions.

—I cooked some leftover meat for you to have with plantains when you get hungry. If I haven't returned, turn on the stove and cook the plantains that I left on the table.

—Yes, mom— answered the boy, still half asleep, while the mother confidently swayed to the tropical rhythm, with her perfectly shaped hips and the sound of her half heel, black moccasins, a purple V—cut skirt that squirmed down to her well—shaped figure, and her white delicate silk blouse. Then she crossed through the small room where she had the three pieces of blue furniture she'd gotten with a stroke of luck.

—There's the old stove, I put it out on the floor, in case you forget about it, and one of the boys bumps into the table and falls on it by accident, God forbid. You're the oldest one left in the house, you know. Keep it clean and safe.

After that, she closed the door and left, letting them sleep half of the morning during their school break. The proper boy didn't break the rules imposed by his mother. He was assigned the post of chef of the house, and he perfectly crafted his skill.

The boy kept his eyes on the two little ones, so they wouldn't go to the streets alone. Their playmates had missed them when they went out to play. Some of kids from the block went to the backyard. The fun started as they played tag, and of course everyone ran as quickly as they could to avoid being tagged. As usual, Tati was excluded from the games her brothers played.

—You are very small— they said to her—. Go to play with your doll.

Tati did not understand the reasons why she was rejected by her brothers. Despite being characterized by age difference and her fragile body, she insisted on enjoying the warm atmosphere that filled the yard, as she ran around in laughter.

The old stove was lit. The young brother in charge of supervising Tati was so happy playing he forgot the hot water bubbling in the metal pot over the stove, on the right edge of the patio. Shouts and laughter were heard everywhere.

24

—Tag, you're it! –someone shouted.

Tati, attracted by the noise and without being able to back away, joins the group to play. As usual, she is completely ignored by her neighbors and brothers.

Suddenly, Tati, standing on the opposite side of the patio, is pushed by a girl running madly to avoid being tagged. Tati falls on top of the boiling pot which sat on the portable stove. A terrible scream echoes over the loud gaggle filling—in the background, under the two leafy mango trees that shaded most of the courtyard.

Confusion rules the air. No one knew where the loud cries were coming from, until they realized that Tati was sitting right inside the hot boiling pot. A stunned silence follows, and is again interrupted by the cries of horror, in anticipation of the astonished looks of the kids present.

Without any knowledge of how or when, Tati is taken from that dreadful scene and lifted off the floor as if by a superior force. In an act of desperation, her red shorts are removed from her body at that moment.

The scared, worried boy runs after the eleven—year—old girl who pushed his sister and sees how she stares perplexedly and speechless as she sees how the layers of skin on Tati's back had welted and burst, exposing the soft tissue underneath it.

When the boy sees the astounded young girl, the boy begins to lose it, and grabs the culprit by the neck, while he shouts:

—I'm going to kill you, I'm going to kill you. You burned my sister, and now you're going to die.

The terrorized little girl begins to scream, still in shock:

—Let me go, let me go. Help me! —she yells.

The neighbors approach the scene, attracted by the desperate cries, and they become puzzled, when they see Tati's raw flesh, as a result of the over 100 degree water that boiled on top of her skin. In response to the reaction of one of the neighbors, the youngest of Tati's brothers runs out to look for the parental guardian of the family.

His responsibility as an older brother had already blended him into the labor world to financially support his home. He worked relatively close by when he heard the boy's nervous voice:

—Run, brother! Tati got burned, run!

The young construction worker places aside his tools and runs alongside the little boy without a word. Both brothers arrive, the older brother takes the little girl in his arms, carrying her upside down to avoid hurting her anymore, as Tati already feels that she is dying from the burning pain that tortures her to the point that she goes unconscious. The boy's narrow legs move through the park, to the place where he finds a vehicle to get to the hospital.

Between tweezers, ropes, salt solutions, cottons, etc., the doctors begin their battle against time to keep the girl alive. Tati's pulse weakens with each passing minute. Her aunt gets home very worried, she lives a few blocks away, and upon hearing the neighbors' stories, she desperately places both hands over her head, without losing composure or the correct articulation of words, she screams:

27

—The girl is dying; the girl is dying. Oh, God, and where is my sister? – She repeats over and over, without finding a clear answer.

Tati's mother arrives to the hospital heart broken. A kind nun directs her to the burn unit, where her child lies. The timely connection to the oxygen tank was very effective. There are parts of herself that are vulnerable to the attack of the smallest bacteria, if bacteria were to enter the body it could be fatal, as explained by the doctor in charge of the Emergency Room. Chunky tears roll down her cheeks at the doctor's prognosis.

—The next seventy—two hours are high risk, madam.

—Doctor, for the love of God, I need you to save my daughter's life. This was not a careless mistake, I assure you, it was not careless -the frustrated woman repeated, with a voice disturbed by her weeping. The hands of the clock stand still, neighbors and relatives come and go, while the mother remains motionless inside the waiting room in intensive care with her daughter.

"My God let these seventy—two hours go by quickly", she repeats.

—The patient has third degree burns and is in delicate condition, but out of danger — said the doctor at last, approaching the mother, who had placed certainty in God's hands that it'd all end happily.

—Nevertheless, madam, I must inform you that the girl will remain hospitalized for her recovery. It is necessary to place her in the unit for the treatment of the severe burns.

—How long, doctor?

—Well, everything really depends on how the tissues respond to the antibiotics we are applying. But everything will be fine, I promise it.

As the tree leaves changed color, the ground saw them descend. Day after day, between white sterilized sheets, Tati received the morning visit of the hospital nuns, who between tweezers and pieces of gauze removed the dead skin from its tissues, until the discovery of raw flesh. One afternoon at lunchtime, after four long months had passed, the nun in white went to Tati's bed, to comply with the provisions of bringing lunch to the patient in her room. Immediately, the nun said:

—Where is the girl that belongs in this bed? — While in a rush, the nun looks in the bathroom, the hallway, until reaching the general dining room, where she finally finds Tati, who —moved by the joy of the in—patient children almost in full recovery— got out of her bed and occupied one of the seats, thus breaking the medical staff rules of receiving food in the room.

When the young, worried nurse went to pick her up, Tati attempted to get up from the seat. However, her skin had stuck to the seat and the blood burst forth from the newly formed wounds, thus delaying the recovery process. All of that for disobeying the unbreakable rules of the staff.

Tati felt that hospital room had become her home, until she once again received the comfort and company of the best mother in the whole universe. She left the unit after she was given strict instructions from the doctor.

Chapter III

And on Tati goes through her metaphysical journey into her interior. She returns to her pleasant childhood. From time to time, a hulking, dark—skinned man with wide nose and a half smile comes by.

They say he's her dad. It was something that she couldn't understand. He was hardly ever there. His presence never stuck for her.

The deep bruises left by the burns and her frail figure were joint in her favor, leaving her exempt from the kinds of physical punishment of the children around her faced.

The first five years of Tati's life pass by as she remains cheerful and fully satisfied in most of her desires; the youngest and the only female in the house.

The sun keeps on rising and setting. Las Palmas Park remains the same, raised as a green point that marks the division between the avenues of Sabana Larga and Estrella Ureña. That, in turn, separated the Ozama

Extension and the neighborhood of Los Mina.

Each dusk you see the pleasant face of a good man who slowly walks towards the shade of a small box, tied to one of the trees and open it. A small television set is exposed that projects striking images in black and white which bring delight to dozens of spectators that sit on iron benches. This is a gift made by the Commander—in—Chief, the President of the Dominican Republic, as a token of generosity to poor families.

After the audience has enjoyed the canned programs, the television set is put away. The audience parades back towards their different destinations satisfied after having had some entertainment. It becomes a customary event that generates an enjoyable public encounter.

One morning, at sunrise, Tati sees the family carefully gathering all the furniture in their house. They end up moving at sunset, and she hears their mother say that for some reason, everything must be carried under the shadow of night.

As the twilight vanished taking with it the last of few rays of the sun, the caravan —loaded with junk and expectations— leaves behind the small house, where part of the family history had been built.

The trip was short, and Tati did not realize how long it took her. Her new destination was approximately ten minutes away from her old house. There she would know her first school, a place she would never forget. The one place she often reminded her mother to take her when she saw her brothers leave every morning.

Tati's great intuition screamed that it was time to affirm her rights to do the things that only she was forbidden from doing. "Why could my brothers run to the park every afternoon after watching T.V.? Why did they go to school every morning and I did not go a single day? Why can they do so many things that I'm not able to?", she asked herself, without finding an answer.

Everything has its time and place. The impatient girl, then, concluded that the time had come to enjoy the same rights as her siblings. The morning begins, promising a pleasant day ahead.

Tati's brothers are ready, with the notebook tucked under an arm, to run to their daily obligation of receiving the sacred bread of learning. Although living in the new house, not far from the previous one, she literally feels excluded from regular everyday life.

Suddenly, she decides to exercise the only option she knew to be heard.

—Hm, hm—the ignored little girl cries.

—Why are you crying, my dear girl? —asks the worried mother as she starts performing daily chores.

—Oh, why are you crying, mommy's little girl?

—I want to go to school with them, I want to go —the girl sobbing, begs her mother.

—Easy, my daughter, don't worry. When you're seven, we're going to take you to school.

—Tomorrow, mom, tomorrow?

—Listen, my girl, you're only five years old, school won't take you in until you turn seven.

—Okay, mom, I will go tomorrow.

—Now come to breakfast, darling, come, I must go out and buy food.

Every morning, in the same point of the universe, the same scene is repeated.

Frustrated by the situation, a light turns on in her mother's brain, lighting her with a new idea. She says:

"I'll talk to my boys' teacher tomorrow; I'll ask them to let Tati sit in a little chair every day. So, she thinks she's at school and she'll stop screaming."

After the mother finished contemplating her great idea, the next day, she took action.

—Good morning, teacher —she hesitates, unsure of what she will propose to the smiling and kind educator.

—Good morning, my ma'am, how can I help you? —he asks in a sweet tone of voice.

— I need to talk to you, professor.

—Tell me, any problem with the boys?

—No, not really. The thing is that I know that the school does not enroll children under seven, but my youngest daughter is only five, you know. She's always crying about coming to school with the rest of the students.

The shy woman doesn't know what else to say. Preschool is a luxury for her current social class, and she knows that. Official costs for school are hardly thought of at such an early age.

—What I ask of you is to let me sit her, with a small chair, at a corner of the classroom, so that she believes she's in school.

—Sure, bring her over, what else can we do— said the teacher with a bright smile.

—Thank you, professor, thank you. God bless you. I will bring her tomorrow.

Chapter IV

It's the moment Tati always waited for. The girl wears a khaki skirt and a little blue collared shirt as the school uniform bought by her mother —yesterday afternoon— in a hurry. The little girl isn't amazed at all, she doesn't understand the achievement accomplished by her mother, she only knows that children go to school and she is a child.

The old house that served as a school is just a few meters away from her new home. The woman takes large leaps on her way to fulfill her promise made to her most beloved treasure; finally satisfied that she found a solution to quite a difficult problem.

She says to her daughter in an enthusiastic tone:

—See, Tati? I told you that you would come to school, and here you are.

The child does not respond either way, since she understands it's the right path to take. But she asks herself: "Why can't I go where others go?"

With just five years of age, she holds half of a small notebook in one hand and half a pencil in her other hand. Tati passes through the open door and places herself inside a part of life she never imagined before and will probably never forget.

It's precisely here, in this place, where Tati has struggled so hard to be in, that she learns from her classmates that she is a "black girl". Her teacher is the most compassionate out of everyone she knows. When she enters the classroom, she sees the smile of a friendly face, a slight image that she will never forget.

—Good morning, little girl, come over here. —He gives her the little table he uses as a desk, placing her at one end of the classroom.

The teacher carries Tati, and sits her, at a view that allows her to see the blackboard, and at the same time separated her from the main group of students who would undoubtedly see her as an anomaly in their group.

The first few hours pass by in peace, recess time approaches and the teacher orders the children to go to the playground to release the energy contained within them. The students run like wild horses and the teacher focuses his attention on his protégé.

—You can go to the playground, little one.

Tati runs to play with the other children. Later, she remains in a state of delight, under the gigantic coral trees that cover in between branches and flowers part of the spacious patio, decorating it with colors and enormous shadows.

She wanders, looking up at the sky, while her baby feet tread on withered petals of red coral flowers, and she keeps going as if nobody's there until she hears someone shout:

—Hey, you, "negrita", get out of here, we're going to start the game.

Tati remains motionless. It's the moment when the team games take place, that attracts her attention and she immediately wants to play.

—Hey, coconut head, move along to the side. You have trouble hearing me?

Yes, she listens, but she can't understand what's going on. She's at the place where she really wanted to be. However, they are calling her "negrita". She was always called by her proper name; it is the one she knows and answers to. Yet, she doesn't comprehend why she is not called by her name, regardless of her skin color.

Amid her confusion, she feels someone pulls her by the arm and shoves her to the side. Her brothers are still in classes, they take their second break in the morning.

She is stands, looking at the point from where she was shoved, and tries to figure out the answers she can't find inside.

After this first day has haunted Tati´s mind there are many others alike to come. She manages to play some of the games at the playground. Even so, the children still identify her by the color of her skin, instead of her given name.

—Come, let's play, with your corn cob hair—they nickname the girl inspired by the four or five sections of the nappy hair that she had inherited from her mother.
—Those guys look at me and they say such strange words to me: "Black crapper, coconut

head, ugly corned hair", the little girl thinks to herself, without knowing any of its meaning, becomes aware of the unpleasantness created from the situation around her, which makes her deduce that she wasn't being complimented, and she announces:

—My name is Tati!

She feels that they make fun of her innocence. The confused little girl can barely fathom that the behavior of the innocent children around her is shaped from a very old culture of racial discrimination. Therefore, everyone at the playground baptizes her with a name that better suits her.

Every day someone makes up new teasing words that symbolize Tati's big eyes, small face, full head of yellowish—red hair, and skinny as a needle. Whenever she hears "daddy long legs", "dagger head", "goat forehead", and a long list of other insults, Tati becomes alert. Even so, she doesn't allow herself to be called anything but her name.

Tati is unaffected, despite the misunderstandings of those who claimed to be her peers. She has no clue if her forehead is large, small, round or square. What she does know, and that instead of flattering those nicknames like "burnt nub", "piece of coal" and others that resonate as insults to her ears, that she begins to dislike.

Her brother "quick—fist" doesn't allow anyone to take advantage of her, although, he isn't always by her side. In turn, the little creature becomes aggressive and daringly takes a stance on anyone who bothers her. Tati is confronted with blows, scratches, hair pulling, etc.

Without measuring consequences or realizing the size or gender of her opponent, she takes on the fight. Since most of the opponents are older than her, of course, she receives more blows than she lands. As a result, this makes her stronger and stronger each day, increasing her inner courage.

One of the nicknames that Tati barely comprehends and bothers her the most is "black crapper". Whenever someone yells those words at her, she goes out to the sidewalk, near the school, to fight with her opponent. She doesn't want the rest of the children to play a role in her struggle for dignity. The sweet teacher comes to recess, and turns bitter, instantly, transforming the playground into no man's land. Tati goes home every day uncombed and disheveled, as a result of her constant fights.

Concerned about the situation, the mother of the injured "black girl", dedicates less time to her usual deeds, and goes to the front of the house to have a view of the school front, from where she waits patiently, until the fight started, which her daughter is doubtlessly involved in. She often runs to the ring, intervening as a good referee.

—You're not going to school anymore, you're too small. I don't know why you fight so much, don't you see that those boys are bigger than you?

—That boy called me a "black crapper" — the aggravated girl replies with puckered lips.

—I want to come to school –she keeps insisting, because she definitely doesn't want to leave school. The place she sees as an equal opportunity for all.

That's the outcome of Tati's first experiences in school. In other words, that's the first bite out of corruption the individual faces. The controversial place where the verbs, formation and deformation of any social entity are combined. There you learn the good, the not so good and the bad, as products of the diverse behaviors from each home.

The favorable percentage of inheritance and world of the well—known Mendel's Law has undeniably taken its course of action, prevalent at each moment and place. Schools are faced with behaviors of which teachers have no control over. Well, what can they do? They're teachers, not magicians. The children are educated by their parents and relatives at the home they were born in. In school, these children develop intellect and freely practice the basic instruction they daily carried.

Each day is worse than the one before, the mother's advice is insufficient to keep Tati out of trouble, thus she assigns Tati's brothers the task of protecting her. Her maternal efforts seemed futile as the outcome remained unchanged. Everyone was focused on their personal toil, and the fights increased even more for the same reasons.

Chapter V

Tati, now the "black girl", used the sweet bread of experience to overcome the unpleasant past of her childhood. Some things change, in the next few years she will officially grow to be the girl to walk the long, wise road of scholars.

Tati finally turned seven years old, and the school had a seat ready, solely for her. She had grown to a small extent, she was still tiny, jumped a lot, ate little, but she was ready to officially enter school. Fighting with classmates was not a barrier to have fun and play at the playground.

Tati was extremely courageous, ready to continue standing up for herself, with a little more practice in street fighting. Her classmates are also her neighbors who go from the place where she started to the house where she is also mocked.

Tired and worried after having been the referee of her daughter's countless street fights, her mother decides to switch scenes.

—We cannot keep sending this girl to that school, there are too many violently inconsiderate boys there. It is better making a little more of a sacrifice, and pay for a private school, where the spoiled kids don't go—said the lady to the eldest son, who played a fatherly role, and agreed with her.

—Okay, find a school to enroll her in, I'll give you the money on Saturday, when I get paid.

—God bless you son, you are a real man. Tomorrow I'll go early and talk to the principal of the school on Third Street.

Fully convinced, the family considered that the change was the best solution for all. Since, the public school educated a socially lower class from poor upbringings. The private school would be a much quieter place for the child. They thought Tati would be better there, and there would be no more fights.

The big day arrived. While her brothers left, on their way to the "small jungle", Tati passed through the sill of the "white door". She walks proudly and cleanly uniformed with a new, shiny pink shirt that goes perfectly with the white tones on it. With four buns, rolled like onions, and a beautiful smile that reflects her inner happiness, the little girl concludes her journey under the fluttering butterflies that rose, inviting her to play while gathering daises on the way.

Tati meets new faces, as she occupies a seat, on the third row of benches of the new school. There is a noticeable difference in this school, of course. To her surprise, at her recent arrival, someone almost whispers in her ear, while looking at Tati's hair:

—Four buns soaked with gas. It makes me angry, ha, ha, ha.

Tati tried to ignore them. She couldn't believe what she was hearing. She had thought about what her mother and her brother were talking about. They said that it would be different there.

—Hey, you hairy corn cob, lend me your pencil sharpener.
—No, I would not lend you my sharpener, and watch what will happen after school, I'm going to mess you up.
—Oh, the "black girl" is brave all right!

Tati, in shame, feels the remarkable difference of the desks, the walls, the ceilings, the uniforms, the teachers and other things, they're different, but the misbehavior of the classmates doesn't change.

At the dismissal of the class, she waits for, but cannot find the bad—mannered boy who mocked her, so she goes home disappointed. The flowers stopped shining for a while, and butterflies were not in her path. She felt great sadness, knowing that only her hard fists silence the racial mockery surrounding her. That's not what she wants; she just wants to be respected just as she is. She is sorrowful about the idea of always using violence against the discrimination that embraced her.

Tati felt that the struggle was hers, she would never be able to imagine, that on the other side of the Atlantic Ocean, two African American men, named Malcolm X and Martin Luther King Jr., of the same caste, are moved by the same cause to raise their voices against social class inequalities, especially racism. Little did she know that is what she is going through as well, Tati uses the only available option to her to defend her rights.

Tati doesn't feel different from those around her, she is no different. Therefore, she doesn't understand the teasing and the bothersome insults of her peers. Tati simply doesn't want to continue listening to these derogatory names. Oh no, she doesn't want that. God created her in his image and likeness, her mom tells her she's beautiful all the time so why can't her peers have the same perspective.

Among tears and laughter, fights and arguments, the years passed. Tati remembers a very special day, among many others. She remembers one day when the neighborhood streets were overcrowded by a wide group of crying people, both men and women shouted something like: "We're finally here, we are hopeless, they killed the Benefactor, what will happen to us? What will happen to our children?" The people knelt, some with their hands on their heads, others with their arms raised, shouted in a chorus incorporated in sorrow.

More than a decade later, Tati asks her mother why all the people were shouting in the street that day. She answered this way:

—That was on May 30, 1961, when we heard the news that the Chief was killed. He was the only president we knew, he had been in power for more than thirty years. For that reason, it was inevitable to think that the world would fall apart, that no one would protect us, ha, ha, ha.
—Oh, well...

Chapter VI

Tati continued to grow and became part of the concurring series of events.

—I already have some money saved up — said the mother to the eldest son. I talked to our neighbor's brother. He is selling a lot in New Village, and he will sell it cheaper to me. We will buy it and build a bigger house, because the boys are growing and need space.

—Good, mom! I'm going to talk to my boss, so he can provide me some materials that he is given when he repairs houses.

—We'll make a big comfortable house, so we do not have to move anymore.

After joining efforts, finally comes the time to savor the comfort. With multiplied spaces and leaving behind the pressure of the monthly rent payment. Everything indicates that the family, from now on, will live better. Being part of a new neighborhood, with an appearance of five years when she is already seven, a little taller, just as skinny, with a thick hair inherited from her mother, Tati exhibits a striking figure. Many children call her Fire

51

Head inspired by the yellow—reddish tone, with a wire texture of her hair.

Now her mother spends more time away from home, her commercial area still belongs to the old sector where they lived. The Puerto Rico neighborhood is a little distant from its old point, a distance that would not be a great obstacle for the mother, to transfer in search of job. Here she has found an old friend who is part of the new neighborhood. Everything works for good, because she has someone close to her who watches her children.

Her expectations have not been in vain, so she gets the support and favors she really needs in the hours of absence at home. There is the neighbor's eldest daughter, for whom it is a kind of entertainment to comb Tati every day after school. The outraged creature usually arrives disheveled by the daily fights, for the defense of her rights to live without being mocked.

About the beginning of the adolescence, the "black girl", believes that the time has come to look different. But she insists on being a playmate of her brothers, in addition to running around the streets without asphalt and the vast patio almost covered by the interwoven branches of passion fruits and granadillos. Tati projected a drastic change of image that logically would bring a remarkable change in her physical appearance.

She had expressed to the daughter of the neighbor the imminent need to show off a figure that would bring the solution of her main problems. While the realization of these changes was coming, everyday life ran its hectic course. Thus, every day, when the lunch hour arrives, the misunderstandings between Tati and her brother are forgotten.

—Sister, eat your food. Look, it's already cold and you haven't eaten yet.

—I do not want food; I do not like to eat.

—Well, I'm going to help you eat—. Pass me your food and stand behind me. Stand with your back to mine. I'm going to chew, swallow it, and it passes by your back, and so you don't have to eat and fill your belly.

—How come, little brother?

—Come on, see, the food goes from my belly to yours through the back.

—Oh, well, eat and pass it to me. Good trick, little brother.

—You see? You are not hungry. Are you?

—Oh yes, you ate for me. Right now I am going to the grocery store to buy bread with salami and eat it. It is our secret.

Between these and other children's events, the day has come when Tati's beloved girlfriend decides to put into practice her hairdressing skills. The girl, who combs her daily, must be her first model by logic, she is the ideal model. Tati's main dream will be realized as a product of her decisive decision.

—Ma'am, let's put a relaxing hair cream on your daughter's hair.

—You are crazy? No, that girl is very little.

—Let me straighten her hair, and you will see. She has a very hard and abundant hair. As it is now, you must pull it strongly to unravel it and that hurts.

—I said no, Miss —said Tati's mother quickly.

—But I use it and see how beautiful my hair is. Let me do it. I can tell the lady in the beauty parlor to sell me a little amount, and I'll apply it on Tati's hair. That hair is going to get a lot longer and smoother, she wants a cut with fringes on the forehead, too. Let me make her pretty, so they will not make fun of her, when she has straight hair.

—No, no, and no, leave the girl like that.

Concluding the dialogue, the woman turned around and walked away from the well—intentioned girl.

Some days after, the neighbor insists again. This time supported by Tati, who really wanted to see her hair straight.

Under the imminent promise that the wire—like hair would become a thing of the past, becoming loose, soft and silky; while decreasing its volume to favor the round face, the mother gives in to the pressure to which she was subjected by the novel beautician and the girl.

The complex of not being able to show loose hair, luxury that is not contemplated in the afro hair will disappear. With approximately eighteen years of age and no experience in the application method of hair straightener, the girl does not waste time to execute her plan, barely accepted by the mother.

The relaxer that was sold to her by the hairdresser contains a high chemical content. Enough to pull the curl to any hair. However, in less than sixty seconds, that product may cause hair to fall in large quantities and severe burns to the scalp.

—Tati, I have everything ready, this afternoon I'll apply the straightening cream.
—Good, I'm going to get pretty.

The wooden chair at one end of the courtyard of the empirical hairdresser's house, a tin of water and an old battered aluminum jug, which was used to pour the water was all that was available to carry out the work. A large piece of clear plastic cap takes the place of the protective cover. Besides the comb stick and a pair of latex gloves, as the hairdresser used. Everything is ready.

On the old chair, a young girl full of emotion, sees realized her great illusion and is ready to cooperate so that the operation is a success.

The inexperienced specialist, ready to put into practice what she had seen her hairdresser do, proceeds to divide Tati's hair into ten sections. She would do better than the hairdresser, of that she was sure, therefore she would change the method a bit for a better result. Once again, the statement that the student exceeds her teacher will be fulfilled.

The girl begins to apply the product on the hair of the neck. After soaking a section well wrapped around it, the hairdresser immediately rinses it, because the mixture is very strong, but she leaves it more time for a better result. Then she continues applying section by section until she reaches the area of the forehead.

—It itches a lot —said Tati.
—Try to bear the pain, so that your hair stays long and beautiful.
—Yeah, but it's burning me.
—It does not matter, hold on.

The almost tortured little girl squeezes her eyes hard to resist, she does not want to spoil the expected results. She thinks of the story that her mother tells when she describes the paternal grandfather she did not know. Yes, he was of Indian complexion and totally straight hair. That's what her new hair would look like. Let's see who is going to say all those ugly names now.

She would look a hair like her grandfather's. She would stand for that cause, of course she would endure the kind of burning, pain, and itching that strongly penetrated her scalp until reaching the same brain.

When she returns to consciousness, she shouts again:
—It burns me up, rinse my hair with lots of water —which the insistent young woman

reacts when she sees a full strand of hair fall as it was rolled up.

—Oh, my mother, oh my mother —she shouts, nervous and frightened. Then she throw jars of water on the innocent girl's head that trembles in pain confusing her cries with those of the neighbor.

—Mom, come help me, Tati's hair is falling — screams the desperate stylist.

Everything becomes confused, assisted now by her mother, the young hairdresser sees Tati's hair all destroyed by the strong mixture. The hairdresser will know that another chemical was contained in the glass container that carried the product.

The moment of anguish grows, once the process of rinsing is finished, the girl, with severe burns on the scalp, retains only the frontal line of the hair that she previously had, that resisted for being the last to which the chemical was applied.

When Tati arrives at her house, with her head wrapped in a towel and face of regret, Tati's mother refuses to believe what her eyes see. The girl then removed the towel that covered the misfortune. A couple of thick tears roll down the lady's cheeks.

—I should not have done it —she only whispered.

The process of recovery from burns is slow. The hair that had survived the hecatomb breaks down little by little. The "black girl" says nothing, thinks nothing, she only feels a pain that she cannot describe, but this does not hinder her from moving on.

Chapter VII

That episode in the life of the little girl marked her path even further. She had no idea what awaited her. After that incident she had suddenly lost an abundant amount of hair.

Tati was bald. She continued losing in the following days the little hair that remained when she got burned by the relaxer. The remaining strands broke off little by little; they were on her pillow, on the comb, in the water after washing. The healing process of the burns on her scalp was slow.

It was a new challenge for Tati. A new element was added to her figure, a kind of total baldness. Even so, Tati tries to keep going, she had lost all her hair, which was like wire, but it was her hair. Much better than nothing.

Life must continue. Luckily, there are not many mirrors around, and that will help her, as she will not have to confront her image frequently. Neither does she imagine that sometime after that event her family would be involved in a difficult situation. It would force them to change their neighborhood again.

Twelve years had passed since the early morning of that February 2, when the little girl was born. Tati remembered that the improvised hairdresser's mother had told her that she had seen her start walking, after she was seven months old. The lady laughed making her story, she said that everyone looked at her as something strange, because of the tiny size that reached that age. It gave the feeling that she was a walking flesh and bone doll. This provoked a reaction in everyone who saw her making a fuss with some other popular expressions.

Already a teenager, the "black girl" had a small amount of hair on the head. That is how she would begin a new phase of her life, in a strange neighborhood, where the boys and girls of her age were totally unknown.

That day, both expected and feared at the same time arrived, it was time to leave for the new place, where she had only visited a couple of times in the company of her brother, who already had a girlfriend there. It was time to change from the Puerto Rico to the Vietnam neighborhood. There her aunt had moved a short time ago, which contributed to her mother's choosing this neighborhood as her new destination.

The truck is ready to transport the furniture, behind remains her house. Tati turns and looks at it with great sadness. There is her first tree that she had planted, right next to the entrance door, which rises beautiful, with colorful leaves and leafy branches.

She never knew what the species was called. She only knew that it was beautiful, and that it did not bloom because its own leaves changed color. They turned from green to white with certain pinks spots, which played the role of flowers.

There would stay her plant ...Very sad, she turns her back and climbs the truck towards her new adventure. She did not imagine that she would ever feel the need to plant another tree. Changing the environment was what interested her the least. She would miss the patio entangled among guavas, passion fruits, and others, where together with the youngest of her brothers, she picked up the dry leaves from the ground. Wrapping them in a piece of paper they formed a cigarette, which they smoked as they had seen their mother doing with the tobacco leaves.

There would also remain her butterflies; the house that, as she heard her older brother say, would be the maternal one forever; her neighborhood friends and playmates; and Pastor Cruz's church, which she attended for her Bible school classes. She did not want to leave her house, but nobody asked her, she just had to obey. The political regime at that time and the adults, who were directing their way, had determined it that way.

Chapter VIII

The arrival in the neighborhood Vietnam was a daily event. The populated neighborhood of Los Mina received them as ones more than those who come and go often. Tati was ready to start her new life. A deep sense of bitterness, a smaller house, the same sky, the same sun, but totally unknown neighbors. The first to approach was the girl who lives across the street, a girl her age and who Tati had ever seen, when she went with his brother to the house of the girlfriend who lived there.

Naturally, their friendship grew little by little, along with a list of new friends in the new place. Some of them, would become very important in her life. The days continue to pass like tree leaves in the fall.

There, in her new world, life gave her the sister who had not given her nature, and who casually sought her in every girl she knew. Carlita, a beautiful and affectionate girl, had wavy hair and very soft, clear skin, very clear, and a thin face, a pretty girl. Both shared an unconditional affection that would last forever.

The fact of living at a very short distance, allowed them to spend most of the time together. Tati was the little friend Carlita was waiting for, because the only girl next door of her age did not share with her, because her mother did not allow her to have friends. Carlita was so enthusiastic about her new friend, that she dedicated herself to touring the neighborhood with Tati and presented her as a sister. The expression "impossible" was heard often.

—How? Your sister? So black? —they asked. To which she, with a certain timidity, responded:
—Yes, she is my dad's daughter.
—Uh, uh—someone whispered.

Between those and other events, time passed. September arrived again, as well as the new start of classes. They had finished the summer vacation, and it was time to go back to school. Already in the new neighborhood, Tati had been greeted with annoying mockery, which of course, she hated. Some of them called her ugly black, pineapple head, coconut head, and many other unpleasant nicknames, now more allegorical to her head, which looked a very small amount of hair, and the color of her dark skin.

Despite the bad experiences, she runs happily to school. She feels that there is a place that belongs to her. Once in the new group, the "black girl" begins to receive the insults to which she was not accustomed, nor will ever want to get used to. Some were already known to her, but she still refused to accept them. Tati does not want to listen more to those denigrating qualifiers, such as bald head, wire head, which emphasize the absence of her lost hair, and the slow and stunted growth she tried to replace in the few recovered follicles.

Tati did not want to be involved in more street fights, not anymore. She was too old to fight with everyone and anywhere. At that time she had already visited the church and had greater understanding of the existence of God, both in the Catholic and the Evangelical churches, Tati has heard that if we ask something of God with much faith, he will grant it to us.

—I do not want them to call me head of pepper again, head of coconut or anything else. I'm going to ask God to make me white, so I'll stop being a "black girl". I will have a very white skin and abundant loose hair.

And that's how Tati enters her room. Once there, she kneels in front of her bed, closes her big eyes and fervently asks: —God, make me white, please I ask you. I do not want to keep hearing so many ugly names, make me white, I beg you. With her hands together, she continues saying:

—God, make me white. I promise you that I will behave well, that I will be good. Make me white, Lord. When I open my eyes, I will not be black anymore. I will be a white girl.

Her room is silent. The minutes pass, she wants to give time for God to work with the change of her skin color and her hair. She needs it. Once the time that she considers enough has elapsed, she brings to her imagination her new figure, very similar indeed to that of a little girl who had been her companion in the previous school.

She imagines a soft and smooth skin, clear as the sun, like that of that girl, caressed by a brilliant and silky hair, so abundant that the mother took her to cut it often on the recommendation of the pediatrician, since the heavy thickness of her hair could affect the back of her neck and cause her health problems, according to what Tati had heard.

"So I will become with the help of God," states the girl.

Tati separates the two thick rows of eyelashes. Shy, in order to leave her eyes uncovered, little by little. The miracle is already done. When she opens her eyes, she quickly directs her gaze while raising her right hand, and...

What a so big disappointment. Tati had not received any miracle, had not changed her color, nor her hair. She feels a great sadness, and thinks:

"It can't be, God did not make me white". Will I have to remain black? No, I will not give up, I will ask God again. Next time I will succeed, I will wait longer and I know that God will make me white".

She was sure that God was doing his miracle. Tati had imagined the face that her friends would put when they saw her white. She also thought about what they would say to her. What would everyone do when she was white? She was just sure it would be good, because she never saw her friends teasing her friends for being white, and for having good hair. "That had to be good", she thought.

Yes, she was worried about her mother's reaction. She loved her being black, she said her daughter was her princess, a gift from God in her life. Anyway, she would talk to her mom and she would understand her. Therefore, she would not back down from her goal. She would become a white girl.

Chapter IX

As every afternoon, Carlita was waiting for her to share the twilight hours. Sitting under the shade of the pine that stood imposing on the right side of the house of her friend—sister. There the two girls held frequent meetings, crystallized without prior agreement. It was as if each one lodged the conviction of a commitment. Two rustic wooden chairs served as a stage, where the carefree creatures shared, without thinking of time.

A small red device, moved by the energy of four round batteries transmitted the voice of a recognized announcer who broadcast the radial news. It was the commemoration of the last civil revolt that the country had suffered.

When Tati listened to the announcer, recalled the episodes lived in the post—war period of April 1965, during which her family was affected due to the constant bombings of projectiles. The geographical location of the Puerto Rico neighborhood was decisive. The area was surrounded by forests, and bordered by the flowing waters of a river at its northern end. That place was favorable for the US Marines to set up war camps in the vicinity of that sector during the civil war.

—I cannot forget how my mom got up at dawn to cook a pot of rice and beans, and a pot with spaghetti.

—She left it ready to run with us, when the helicopter passed announcing with a loudspeaker that people had to leave the area.

—Why?

—Oh, Carlita, and where you lived, they did not do that?

—No.

—Ah, they did that for people who lived there to go somewhere else, because the area was in danger in the trajectory of the projectiles.

—How come? Oh God, Tati, and what did you do?

—My mom grabbed the food, entered the pots with spaghetti and the rice with beans in a knapsack, and ran with us to my uncle's house, over there in the park.

—We went back at night, and the next day the same thing was repeated; sometimes we did not have to leave because the helicopter did not pass.

—Wow! We lived in the countryside at that time.

—Ha, ha, ha, my mom went to the farm with us when they overthrew the government of Juan Bosch, because she said that a revolution was going to start. We spent more than a year living in the countryside, and since there was no war, my mother returned, and shortly after returning the war began.

—What a bad luck.

—I remember that there was once, that we did not have time to get to the uncle's house, and Mom knocked on any door on the road. There they let us in and we had to camp until the attack passed. There they shared the saddlebags that my mom had reserved for the day. That morning I had made a rice with salami, and she shared it with the people of that family, who opened their doors to us in such a difficult moment—. But do not think that only that happened...

—Tell more, what else?

—Hey, listen to what happened then to my cautious uncle. He came to live in the Capital in the mid—fifties. After spending several years and building two cottages, he ended up considering that the city was very busy, crowded, and scandalous. There was very much running around for his taste. The advice of his sisters was in vain. He did not mind leaving these properties behind and returning to Los Llanos de Pérez with his family, where he was from, and he should never have left, he said.

He was very calm; he detested the bustle and the movement of the metropolis; he only visited the city of Santo Domingo to collect the rent money he received for the small houses, and to greet his sisters who lived there.

But destiny touches you when it's your turn, the uncle had come to visit on April 22, 1965, just two days before the revolution that took place in the Plaza de Los Trinitarios, at the head of the Juan Pablo Duarte Bridge. And just on the 24th, in the early hours of the morning, accompanied by the eldest of his nephews, the uncle had crossed to Duarte Avenue, only four blocks from the bridge. His goal was to do some shopping for his return trip the next day.

It was just the moment when the outbreak of the war started, almost on his feet. My brother would then tell how he passed a lot of difficulties to get to his sister's house where he stayed on each trip. There was no active transport as a result of the conflict and they had to make the long journey walking, harassed by the thrill sound of bullets. While running soaked in their own saline waters, one asked the other "Am I alive?" feeling the uncertainty that they would never return to the sweet home. Thus, the uncle was forced to live all the ravages of the revolution in the Capital. Then we would see him sitting in a corner with slight movements, as if he were a human rocking chair, just whispering:

—Look, I do not live in the Capital for the trouble they provoke, and notice how this war took me here without can go home.

Several times he was seen with his hands on his forehead, pensive and crestfallen, lamenting his fate and counting the days waiting for the revolt to cease and could return to the peace of his home, where he should not have left that day.

—I imagine he never came back here.
—You're right, he did not return to the Capital for many years.

The days of the revolution passed, the country entered a stage of moral and economic recovery. By 1966, Dr. Joaquín Balaguer assumed power. He had been elected by the people to recover the democracy lost after the overthrow of the constitutional government, presided by

75

Professor Juan Bosch, in September 1963. That period of Dr. Balaguer lasted for twelve years, was called by some sectors a bloody period for the country.

At that time there was a series of very strong political persecutions against the opponents of said regime. Among these opponents ended up joining the two brothers who preceded Tati, who were already around the age of majority and for one reason or another identified with the causes, advocating against that system of repressive government.

Under an atmosphere of social imbalance like the one that was lived, added to the repression of the government, the children of the house took to demonstrating in disagreement with the regime of Balaguer and his uncontrollable forces, as he called him in his public speeches.

As expected, this resulted in the three brothers who lived in the house being identified as communists opposed to the government. That was almost a death sentence for anyone.

The police at that time had official orders to physically persecute and eliminate opponents, or communists as they were called, locked in prisons, and then disappeared.

It happened that one night during a lightning mobilization, they called it to the act when a group of five to six young people appeared suddenly, stationed in the shadows of any dimly lit corner in one of the surrounding neighborhoods. In lightning action they burned a pair of old tires and some replica of the American flag, in protest to the invasion or intervention of the Yankee Marines of April 28, 1965.

That night, the brave young men were caught in the action of protest, and the one who had the least skill to disappear into the alleys was one of Tati's brothers.

The rookie protester was arrested and then taken to La Victoria prison, accused of communism and opposed to the regime. The good–natured and new revolutionary, had the fortune of being one of those who came out alive from there, after having spent ten months incarcerated, in the prison that does not make honor to its name.

From those facts, the family was the victim of the tenacious persecution that brought therefore the inescapable option that the fifty—year—old lady renounced the house she had built, with the intention of turning her into the maternal house for life.

Her family was the most important thing, and they could not continue living there. She was terrified from the moment when, at nightfall, the police officer from a nearby barracks approached her to give the humble mother a friend's advice. The uniformed officer said, without making up the words:

—Keep the secret, but if you want to keep your children alive, you must get away from here. Your house is constantly being watched by the police. I tell you this because I know how you have raised your children working hard.

—Don't worry, officer, I appreciate your consideration —replied the mother, without leaving her amazement...

That was how the warned woman shed the property she had built with such sacrifices. She was only heard saying that the most important thing for her were her children. She did not care about anything else. She sold her house to get them away from such a strong threat.

She sold it to the first bidder who offered to buy it. That is how they went to live in the Vietnam neighborhood, after assuring the commander that she would go far away with her children.

Tati, of course, was part of the package and began a new phase of her life there. In her new habitat, where the stage also led her to the conclusion that it was better to be a "white girl". Undoubtedly, people are the same everywhere.

Chapter X

The modest mother did not fail to proudly present her little princess. Often, many adults flattered her saying: "How slender is that brunette, and what a nice body she has"; or they said "God bless your daughter, that girl has a beautiful body. Although she is black, she is pretty". "Why did they have to tarnish the compliments at the end?" Tati asked, without getting an answer. That contributed to weigh more mockery than those flattery, which anyway ended opaque.

As the hands of the clock do not stop, as the days passed, Tati's social role grew. Most of her friends were very light skinned. Among them, she remembers with great affection the Sang brothers. Their relations of friendship were very special, particularly with Irma and Sonalis, daughters of an Asian father and a Dominican mother of extremely "white skin; they and their two brothers were the product of a genetic cross that was very well achieved. The four boys were endowed with a very good physical appearance that combined with the good education received, made each of them an excellent person.

Irma, the eldest of the sisters, always gave great respect to Tati, thus becoming part of the small group of her unconditional peers.

Tati appreciated that these girls had white skin, long, soft, silky hair that waved below her waist, like delicate sheets of seaweed reflected through the waters. Their eyes looked half torn, contrasting with the defined lines of the body punctuated by the charm of the Latin curves inherited from the mother. They were possessors of all those attributes of what is called physical beauty. Tati never heard degrading or racist expression that came from them, as should be natural, instead of the exception. The young Tati knew how to value this friendship, which sadly would fade with the passage of time; oppressed by the few communication channels of the time. The Sang family migrated to New York City. It was the time when communication was very limited, which contributed to the fact that after some letters and just a vacation trip of the brothers, the shared walks and longing, especially with Irma in that stay, marked a farewell that time would extend indefinitely.

The daily life was still hard for the still black girl. However, she was sure it would change. Tati maintained her faith in the future, regardless of the hostilities that her life played. Among many others, also emerged in her trunk of memories, one of the most relevant experiences of her existence.

Tati attended the art classes of the school, when one day the teacher of this subject came up with a play that would be presented in the celebration of an artistic act to the mothers. Professor Vitini chose a group of girls to stage a small drama, which was inspired by a Negroid poem.

The most interesting thing of all was the name of the work, "Romance of the black girl", authored by the Argentine poet and writer Luis Cané.

She did not care about the author's purpose. The only certain thing was that Tati would be part of the group chosen for the dramatization of it. Preliminary arrangements began, Professor Vitini would choose the participants in the work... Suddenly, the skilled teacher arranged:

—Tati, you will be the black girl.
—I, teacher?
—Yes, you.

Tati lowered her head and remained silent. The teacher was not contradicted. She was the chosen one. Why her? No, she did not want to be the "black" girl, but nobody asked her. She only received the order. Her opinion did not count. Tati did not have an opinion.

There were other dark—skinned girls in the group, of course, but the darkest was her. At the beginning of the rehearsal a scene is created where a group of fair—skinned girls play happily. They all have fun, but they ignore the "black" girl. They do not play with her. According to the teacher, the "black" girl must stay out of the group, lonely, with a sad face and dressed in white, begging a glance.

In another part of the drama, Tati must kneel with great sadness reflected in her face, while the conglomerate of the six girls made up of her companions, pointed her with the index finger.

The teacher, of cinnamon skin, is narrating the happy poem. All the white girls sing, and point their finger at the place where Tati stays, while listening to their scream in chorus "the black girl cried."

The first trial is running. Tati, locked in her misfortune, only thinks: "And this is what awaits me in life? Why that one must be me? Well, no, I'll see how they'll do if God makes me white before the day of the play. I'll see who will play my role. Today I'm going to ask God to make me white again. I know that God will make me white. I know that I will not have to present myself in public, on the day of the assembly, as that black girl. You'll see, you'll see."

Chapter XI

The first rehearsal is over. The girl undertook her daily walk, descending in the middle of the two rows of houses, on both sides of Central Street. Without perceiving the movements around her, Tati accelerated more and more her steps, firm and determined to end once and for all with that situation. It's the usual time when nobody is home. Her mother remains immersed in her daily tasks outside the home, and her brothers were focused on their own things. Her older brother had already set up a separate home, procreating his own family. Once inside the small room, which she shares with her mother, she kneels again.

Knelt in front of the bed, Tati closes her eyes and thinks "God did not make me White the last time I begged him, because I opened the eyes too fast. I did not give him time to turn me white. Today I will wait longer, and when I open my eyes, my skin will be white.

Thus, Tati repeats her prayers repeatedly.

— Lord, I'm going to keep my eyes closed until you make me white. Please, I beg you... I do not want to remain "black". I don't want to be in that play like the black girl. I do not want to be sad and despised by all, I do not want to be ignored by my color, just for being black. I didn't choose to be black. I don't want to be black. So I'll be here until you make me white.

Tati allows time to elapse. The lamp on the bedside table and her scattered things in the small room, are silent witnesses. She keeps her eyes closed and the same position. Knelt faithfully, Tati considers has passed enough time for God works in her case.

Now she is ready to meet her new skin color, Tati thinks again. "When Mom arrives and sees me, I'll tell her that God made me white. When she sees me, she won't recognize me, and I'll look more beautiful."

Tati knows that her mother adores her, and that she presented her to her friends as her greatest treasure, just as she was, dark skin, almost hairless, no matter what her forehead was like. She and her older brother always bought her beautiful dresses in organdy fabrics, embroidered with laces, and bright leather shoes. Now, as a teenager, being white she would look better.

Tati plunges back into those thoughts as time goes by. She needs to put her ideas in order, because she will have to face everyone before her imminent change. So, it's time to open her eyes, it's been a while.

—God, it's over! —Tati unfolds her eyelids little by little, very slowly, she must control her emotions, because she already has her new skin.

Without being able to avoid the bliss of her emotions, she lets in a slight reflection of light through only one of her eyes. Still bristling, she does not want anything to disturb the special moment. When she opens her first eye, she finds the big surprise... She was still black. She could not believe it, nor accept it. She was sure that everything would change from that moment.

The tiny little woman, gets up crestfallen, feeling that God has failed her. She had heard so many times that God answered the prayers; therefore she would not give up.

—I will not give up, I want to be white—. She would continue to wait for her desired change.

However, life does not change its path, and thus the beautiful and revered day becomes the terrible day of the act to the mothers for Tati.

Everything is carefully organized for the presentation. At the end of the assembly hall is the wooden platform, and on top of it, almost cornered on the right, the microphone that will reproduce the voice of the teacher. In front the rows of chairs that will serve as seats for the ladies who will receive such a worthy tribute.

In addition to the drama, there will also be songs and poems. Poems like that of the Indio Duarte entitled "I consent everything to you, except disrespect my mother." And others artistic pieces, which highlight the qualities and abnegation of a mother.

On the far left hang the folds of the red curtain that will be rolled before and after each participation. Tati, who has not been able to escape to her "protagonist" role, is there feeling an unpleasant emotion of bitterness in her throat, knowing she was ordered to act.

She must obey, there is no option, the elders decide, and period. The teachers are the second parents, therefore the "black" girl was subject to do her duty regardless of her opinion.

The young teacher, of very beautiful and delicate figure, skinny, cinnamon skin, thin face, and slightly curly hair, which enhances her elegant and respectful image, is ready to debut with her cast. Until that moment, Miss Vitini had liked Tati a lot, but from now on, it would not be the same, since she would see her as the main responsible for the bad moments that the indignant little girl is going through.

The act has begun. The afternoon looks splendid. The time of the drama arrives. The curtain opens. The young lady, microphone in hand, begins to sing the notes of the poem. The girls, very well trained, occupy the place indicated before on the stage. Tati is standing in the place that stages the door of the house where the black girl lives. The girls in the neighborhood played on the sidewalk. The other girls in the neighborhood never played with her. All dressed in white, starched and composed, in a silence without tears, the black girl cried.

The white girls chosen to stage the other part, play and laugh out loud and when they hear the teacher's pause, they all sing to the unison the last part of the stanza: "the black girl cried". They also shout and point out at the same time to the rejected girl.

Tati, in her position, feels outraged while she is the target of the tip of each index that wounds her interior, as an accurate firing of rifle in a battlefield. They are all those innocent little hands the living expression of a camouflaged discriminatory inheritance. Her little friends do not even imagine how Tati's dignity, pride, and feelings are hurt.

While for Tati the worst thing of all is that within that group that points her out and choreographs the refrain rehearsed ... There, just a few steps away, pointing with her index finger, is her faithful little friend, Carlita, the clear skin girl who had insisted on calling herself her sister.

Tati will never forget the image of her beloved friend, her sister, despising her in that drama, only because she is "black". Yes, her little friend. She only obeys instructions, but Tati does not assimilate it this way, she is her sister, and period. She should not be there pointing and despising her; this multiplies her pain.

The show continues, amid applause and laughter. Tati really feels dying, until at last the voice of the teacher is heard saying:

"All dressed in white, starched and composed, in a pine coffin, rests the black girl."

The girl must remain lying on the floor, simulating being dead, while the other girls chant, pointing out with her finger at the alleged corpse.

—The black girl rests.

The minutes are eternal at this moment for Tati. The drama develops successfully, while her soul agonizes. Only when she hears the applause of the audience, Tati feels her soul returning to her body.

Finally, the curtain is closed, this means that she can get up from the cold and hard floor where they confined her. Then she runs to the dressing room and remove that horrible white wardrobe that identifies her as the "black" girl.

"But who said there are black girls? To whom could such a barbarity occur? Girls are girls, period.," Tati thinks as she slips between them to walk home without anyone noticing.

All are entertained with the novel poet who now occupies the stage, the show continues and that favors her to disappear from the place. Even so, Tati never cried for those reasons, because she was sure that crying would not change anything. She only cried when she wanted to manipulate her mother to scold her brother when she considered it fair. Yes, fair, because she understood that justice is paramount in daily life.

Chapter XII

Time passes, Tati is reaching the dreamed of teens years; she is no longer the little girl who a few years ago coincided in her struggles with the great icons of equal rights in other scenarios.

Literally, she was motivated by strong personal reasons. Reasons that from the other end of America, had also contemplated recognized activists, like the African-American Malcolm X, and the illustrious American pastor Martin Luther King. They had raised their voices from different points of view and other forms of struggle, but for the same feelings. The so—called racial differences would continue to be the main reason.

Their struggles were deployed in pursuit of equality. Tati fought with anyone who did not see her properly. Only with the aim of being called by her name like so many others, and not with nicknames of racial discrimination; but she realizes that her street fights have not solved anything.

She had a thousand reasons to be happy, therefore, despite her long struggle, she always keeps a beautiful smile on her face that much love.

Each time, she is more flattered among those around her. The mother and brothers of Tati, spare no effort to please her tastes and needs almost one hundred percent. Although the economic level of that family is not one of the best, it does not qualify among the worst, from the oldest to the smallest, they take care to fulfill her needs.

Tati remembers that since she began to feel the soft breeze of Christmas, happiness multiplied magically. She lived with great enthusiasm every minute from the middle of the month of October, until February, because for her Christmas culminated with the celebration of her birthday.

The dressmaker of the neighborhood was in charge of making each dress that she would wear during the holidays. Tati longed for how beautiful it was in those days to run everywhere waving her skirts raised by the cretonne that gave her a princess look. She looked wonderful in her pink dress in organdy, with the white shoe and pink socks, on December 25th.

It was amazing to see her in that yellow dress with fine applications at the edge of the neck and sleeves, the special touch of the string tied to the waist, combined with patent leather shoes and white socks, which color symbolized good luck for the rest of the year, according to her mother. The soft yellow of her dress and the big ribbons or headbands that adorned her head, made her feel excited at the arrival of a new year.

This gave way to the premiere of the tender blue dress with honeycombs on the bodice made in organdy or nylon. It was her Kings Day dress. That part of her life had made her especially happy year after year. She remembered, instead, that her birthday dress varied in color each year, according to her choice.

The magic of Christmas was unique. A soft and caressing cool breeze set the sunsets. The multi—colored lights, the dry branches rolled with cotton, turned into cute little trees, garlands and bells, added to the music that identified those special days. The sound of the bells of the church that announced the march of the early morning bonus.

Everything gave meaning to the large table that, lying in the center of the room, served as a bed to the usual roast pork, salads, cakes and, of course, the well—seasoned and tasty spaghetti were never lacking.

It was so pleasant to know that accompanying the delicacies of those tables there would be grapes and apples, nuts and hazelnuts. They were special snacks, as many will remember that they were only imported to Dominican Republic for the Christmas holidays. They had to wait for an entire year to eat an apple, what made that delicious fruit be more appreciated Three Kings Day was celebrated every fifth of January, and gave the best color to Christmas. A little grass accompanied by a couple of mint candies and a glass of water, guaranteed the arrival of new toys. The lower part of the children's beds became the special stock after the visit of the wise men, the three kings, in the silence of the night.

Already in adolescence, everything was past. Leaving behind the ground that saw her grow up, she was not a child anymore. She was still black, and the interested looks of children of her age and even the oldest ones began. With new names incorporated into her list of friends, Tati had met Maly, a beautiful young girl with big brown eyes, a well—designed nose, clear skin, and a long and abundant hair that made her look beautiful. Maly, like Irma and Carlita, always showed Tati a special affection, also presenting her as her sister in most of the occasions.

Despite the passage of time, society remained the same. The immolation of those great heroes and heroines, who gave everything for the cause had served little. Tati's hair is still scarce, because she has not managed to recover the volume of hair lost. Already stand out well—fitted booty, thin waist and a natural grace to smile that catches the attention of everyone.

Outside the school there is also a whole world full of irregularities, popular music shines at the expense of mocking the black and the ugly ones, nouns that for many are synonymous.

Currently a merengue sounds sentencing all "blacks" to be used for oil, adding one more element for teasing. Although the merengue orchestra is composed of a group of black—skinned members, people took it to heart, and that chorus was popularized with great enthusiasm and an irrational kind of satisfaction, for all those who enjoy mocking the "blacks". It does not take long to wait, at any time someone screams at the presence of a person with a high concentration of melanin.

—Tati can give a good oil. Ha, ha, ha —the mocking laugh resounds.

It is not the only thing that happens to her when she walks through the busy streets of the neighborhood. In addition, another hit parade sounds inviting to eliminate the ugly ones. And while some produce certain money with their musical successes, others have fun highlighting the lack of attributes of "beauty", as described by an anonymous composer.

"Run, they are going to eliminate the ugly ones".

That is the theme of another popular song in those times, a motivation for those who considered themselves white to punch blacks´ faces.

For a long time said songs remained in the great preference of the public, almost considered national anthems. All these experiences led Tati, although she was not so young, to remain committed to her goals that

God would make her white. She wouldn´t give up. She knew she would make it.

While that moment came, she had to continue facing the offensive expressions of those who considered themselves "white and beautiful". Worse still, even of other "blacks" who overturned their frustrations by rubbing the notes of those songs to another subject of the same skin color. Are those jokes supposed to be funny? Is it expected that the person alluded to feel flattered and smile happily?

"It had to be a black person", was one of the irritating popular expressions used to reproach unpleasant behaviors. Tati could not give credit to such expressions, because if a black person does something similar, no one says he or she had to be white, but he would say, you are thinking like black, or a black one always make mistakes at beginning or at the end of any task. She did not understand why —if everyone is reckless occasionally— only black people are criticized that way.

Tati wondered who would be the person that after Creation called whites to the beautiful, precious ones, a group of individuals only considered superior to anyone for having a different skin tone and a different hair texture.

No matter how many questions the girl asked herself, she simply did not find answers. Did not Tati find them, or were there really no such answers? She had not yet read about the history of Adolf Hitler, or about so many other cases of horror and who executed them. Apparently, there was no need, she felt that something did not fit well in society.

Calling blacks, ugly, horrific and other denigrating adjectives and subject to constant discrimination to anyone who does not enter the line. If there are not two equal individuals on earth, why not accept that each one is simply unique and unrepeatable.

Chapter XIII

The world lived the yearned era of the seventies, innocence lasted until very early age. The frequency of the compliments grew, as well as the manly looks from very handsome young people. They whispered constantly phrases like "I want you to be my girlfriend". "If you look at me, I will be the luckiest man in the world". "I can wait for your acceptance, for as long as you want". They expressed young girls between seductive phrases with different words, but similar intentions.

These new components made the confusion grow in that small bud that unfolded its petals to become a beautiful flower. Regardless of its color, a flower in bloom is always a beautiful flower.

Even the compliments of young people, not so young and old, made Tati feels something different, the expressions mocking the color of her skin resounded more in her ears and in her feelings, even when they were addressed to others of the same condition as her. The great attraction that already aroused in the opposite sex, and the many expressions of flattery, even of people of their own sex who stood out with admiration, the gifts of her contoured figure.

All highlighted the defined lines of her waist and hips, the well molded of her raised booties to the point that many said they were perfect and that they seemed handmade. Admiration grew. For her, all those compliments remained unnoticed.

The mockeries so bothersome that had invaded her since childhood, have convinced her that she was ugly. Those were the reasons why she, the "black" girl, would remain firm in her goals that God would make her white.

Chapter XIV

Everything has its time and its hour. We must know how to wait. The young girl has waited long enough.

"It's the third time I'm going to do it, I know he will not fail me," thought Tati. When the time comes for her next and last encounter with God to make her white, she will raise her prayer one more time.

The girl is sure that God will not fail her. She always heard that the third one is the winner. This is the day when everything will change. It is obvious that with the compliments she receives for the body that God gave her and a white skin color she awaits from him, she will look like the perfect girl she dreams to be.

Once inside her room, Tati kneels before the image of her redeemer. She repeats repeatedly, very convinced, "Today God is going to make me white, I know, I feel it. I no longer must hear those horrible and humiliating things to which I have been subjected."

Tati, with a special smile drawn on her small lips, squeezes her big eyes tightly, while exclaiming with all devotion:

—God, beloved Lord, king of the world and our father, I ask you to make me white. Lord, I ask you that when I re—open my eyes, whether I am white, very white, or just a little white, it does not matter, but that I may be white.

—I want to be white! —Tati shouts from the depths of her interior, and in the privacy of her bedroom.

She is willing to get what she needs so much to stop feeling mocked. The black girl is willing to wait for as long as it takes for God to do his work. It will not happen like the last time; no, today she will wait.

Maybe half an hour had already passed, who knows. Suddenly she feels a chill that invades her body, her skin bristles from her feet to her head. "My skin is changing," she thinks.

While she opens her eyes, with her face held high, Tati feels happy, the Lord has done her miracle.

"Now what will everyone say when they see me again? I am already white", she smiles looking up the tin roof.

She knows that it is a unique moment, she wants to wait before looking and touching her new skin, her arms, her hands, her feet and all her white body. Logical, she is totally beautiful. Everyone said that her face was fine, her eyes big and her lips small. Although she did not like her nose, her body is almost perfect. The only problem was "the black skin". Now she expected to look like a special figure, like an icon lowered from heaven.

—It was time already, ha, ha, ha, ha. That's over —repeats the girl over and over again.

Already ready to enjoy with her eyes the new color of her skin, Tati gradually lowers her gaze, and suddenly explodes in screams...

—Nooooo, nooooo, it cannot be possible, what a disappointment, I cannot believe it! It's not true, I felt when God made me white! I felt it!
—I felt when my color changed —she repeats, lowering her sad face—. How would I continue to bear being black? How?

Suddenly a thought assails her, and she smiles.

—Maybe I'm already white, but I'm looking the same. Sure, I felt my change, I'm sure, and I'm not black anymore. I'll wait for others to see me and see what they tell me. I'll wait...

Then, Tati stands with new expectations. Go out to the street. She goes to the Carlita´s house, who, upon seeing her, will surely confirm the change.

"Carlita will be amazed to see me." Quickly she crosses and reaches the five hundred meters that separate her from her little friend. Once there, Tati calls Carlita with great insistence:

—Carlita, Carliitaaa, where are you? Come over here.

—Wait, I'm taking a shower.

—Well, I will wait until you finish — murmurs Tati.

A few minutes pass and the other girl finally leaves from the bathroom, where she threw a few jars of water, collected in an old metal container. The precious liquid is very scarce in the neighborhood and nobody can afford to waste it.

Carlita, still wrapped in the old and faded towel, directs her steps to the room where the black girl is. When she sees her, asks:

—Tell me, Tati, is something wrong?
—No, I came to see if you were here.

Saying this, she lowers her head once again, disappointed. Her dear little friend had not seen her white. That means that God did not please her."

Tati concealed her sadness. A great weight fell on her shoulders and without making any reference to the subject, kept an attitude as if nothing happened. She did not find a way to explain why she was there, at her friend's house. She preferred to remain silent.

Chapter XV

It took Tati a long time to get over that moment. Life did not lose its meaning. Her friends from the neighborhood showed her great affection all the time. They all kept growing together in harmony.

The third of her brothers had become a teacher at the elementary school in the neighborhood. Driven by the desire of progress of the youth in the seventies, he and other talented young people from the neighborhood founded the Club Lovers of Progress, of which he was its first president. Their fervor and enthusiasm made their ideas a source of culture and social development, where Tati had the opportunity to face her stage fear.

Tati enjoyed and participated in all the activities that took place there. The fact that two of her brothers were at the head of the club, gave her freedom, with the consent of her mother, to participate in the constant festivities, beach tours, and social activities that took place there.

Family parties and watching movies were the entertainment of the youth of the time. The boys fell in love then by means of small messages that they wrote and sent to the girls with some of the children that surrounded them. Living even within a strict control of the patriarchal system, Tati enjoyed the shadow of her brother to make possible her participation in all the activities, since her mother would not deny her permission, because he would be there.

Her group continued to grow, and the girl's self—esteem increased. Without understanding why, the number of suitors increased every day. Now the black girl is constantly courted by young men, and even by some of her own sex. Most of her lovers were handsome and elegant. And even, ironically, those who identified as white men.

In the classroom she was always classified in the select group of the smartest. Her grades were excellent, without exerting much effort. Her classmates argued to integrate her into the teams of research works, since she was considered a bright student.

Tati completed her academic tests and usually supported her classmates by telling them the answers they were missing. She knew that she was running the risk of being discovered and disqualified from the tests by her teachers. But that never bothered her, because the most important thing for her was to be able to help, and that everyone around her reached a good final grade.

Tati's mother, fearful of the political repression suffered by the students of the seventies, insisted on the young girl to leave school since she made the middle school.

The good lady claimed that she already knew how to read and calculate, so it was not necessary to continue secondary studies, as the students were persecuted during their protests, and they were often shot at the hands of the police, by order of the current government.

Restless in her aspirations, the girl did not stop a single moment the march towards her uncertain future, although she continued to listen as the people of color were mocked. She thus complemented her studies with several technical courses, available then.

The technical courses taught in those time were typing, filing and shorthand. She also studied cosmetology. This allowed her to experience the satisfaction of embellishing and transforming the physical appearance of thousands of women who passed through her hand in the exercise of the profession, and which she always alternated with other areas of her working life.

The juvenile romances gave special meaning to all those stages of Tati's life. Romantic songs, poems and serenades. Awakening in the middle of the night, lulled by the delicate sound of the thin strings of the guitar, expressing the admiration that aroused the splendor of her tender smile, which could not be extinguished by the unconscious discriminatory behaviors, inherited from the almost natural relative environment with Mendel's law. She always enjoyed the fact that being in the company of her group of friends considered beautiful, she attracted the insistent male glances and manly compliments, as if the physical beauty was entirely reflected in her figure.

Higher education and the working world opened their doors to the black girl. However, there was no lack of someone from time to time to remind her that she was fine, pretty and with a well–defined figure, but that she was black, using the consoling expression:

—You are very pretty, the only drawback is that you are black.

—I don't mean to be rude, sorry.

—Me either.

—Black people are good food for pigs.

—At least we are good for something, others do not eat pigs –Tati answered to the mocking ones.

Meanwhile, she had some opportunities in the workplace. Tati began to work in the maintenance area, and from there she climbed to the administration area, where she oversaw part of the company's accounting. She never thought twice to take the next step, she kept going always forward.

Her work skills were praised by both her colleagues and her administrative staff. This led her to several job promotions in the institution, to which she belonged for a long time. She did not want to stop there, despite her achievements. Her ambition would take her forward, because she planned to move to a much larger company. Although the feelings to achieve were still latent, the negative events tended to overshadow, but not to the point of completely blocking the personal disposition to socialize. Therefore, the friends of her childhood always maintained a very special place in her life, and at every moment they were present, especially her friends Maly and Carlita.

Chapter XVI

After the stage of the first kiss, the marital commitment had touched the doors of her excited heart. That fortuitous encounter with the handsome gallant of her dreams took her there. It was time to leave the warm bed with a maternal aroma to inhabit the convulsive sheets of the passionate bed to which Cupid leads. When this moment arrived, Tati set out on the endless path that she would follow her beloved.

—I feel he is my prince, Maly, I'm twenty years old. I am madly in love. He is a handsome, elegant, educated, loving young man, with great ability to consider any small details to please me. What else I can ask for?

—That's true, and more with how crazy he is for you. I am sure that both of you will be very happy.

—Do you remember how we met him, Maly? You were with me that day, ha, ha, ha.

—I remember, that meeting was so special, you fell in love immediately.

—I think so, ha, ha, ha, since he spoke to me on the phone that day, without imagining his face, I loved his voice, and then it turned out that we studied at the same university.

—And to complete the positive things, his mother worked at the same place than you, Tati. Too many points in common, considering the way you met.

—It really was a lot of coincidence, if I add to all that, how beautiful he was, his tall stature, light brown eyes, his light complexion and his beautiful smile, but above all the love he felt, I did not question his love anymore. I threw myself into his arms.

—The good thing is that in your house they accepted him, and they accepted you in theirs.

—Definitely he had so many attributes. He melted me with those serenades with which he awaked me up at dawn. Ah, how exciting was to wake up listening to the sound of the strings of a guitar and the whisper of his voice with those songs by Camilo Sesto, which sounded more beautiful when he sang for me. I did not know if it was because I fell in love, but I thought he had the voice of an artist. It is a shame that after that he only brings me serenades when we are upset.

Thus they decided to unite their lives in a single space, and without demanding more than they had at their disposal.

As the saying goes, it is not the same together as scrambled, and the marital relationship under one roof was quite fleeting. In just a few months the newly built dream empire collapsed. From that beautiful story was born her first child.

She was satisfied as a mother, but she got divorced. She was bachelor again. The incompatibility of characters was stronger than both could dominate.

Tati then had a new reason to try harder every day, and to work and study in search of a better future. She always maintained the unconditional support of her mother and her brothers.

—I love coming to this place to have coffee with you, Maly. I like to see the twilight from here, it serves as inspiration to do a kind of introspection.

—You know, Tati, you are my best confidant. By the way, I still do not assimilate that you separated so soon.

—Well, Maly, I prefer a healthy separation than to maintain a relationship based on a macho ideal for a long time. I do not consider that the man can keep living his life like a single person, without responsibility. He needs to support his wife, to treat her as his partner.

—Tati, but it's amazing that your matrimony lasted so little time.

—Well, Maly, I told him more than once that I've never seen anyone go before a judge to marry themselves. As a matter of logic, there are always two. That must mean that there are two people who renounce singleness to share another lifestyle. Therefore, it does not correspond that of the two, one follows the life of single and the other married.

—That's true.

—It's not that I think it's easy, it's just preferable. If you cannot, you cannot and period. You must go ahead and then give yourself another opportunity, but of course, with another person, not with the same man.

—I think you should return. You know, you have a son that must be taken into account.

—We must not make the same mistake that others make, the children can have a worse time living under a dysfunctional union, between dislikes, fights, cries, disappointments and disagreements... Oh, and the worst of all is to be used and involved in the problems of the couple. That brings, by all extremes, children full of frustrations.

—I think so, I still have not seen that work.

—I don't accept advises otherwise. I prefer to be alone than badly accompanied.

With an extension of herself in her lap, she undertook the search for new horizons in pursuit of an economically and emotionally stable life, now with more effort than before, since it is her job to ensure a fair standard of living for her beloved son.

God had given her that blessing of being the mother of a child who depended one hundred percent on her, and she would never fail him, because he would follow her example, she would repeat herself again and again.

Following each step that life marked for her, Tati, the black girl, took new directions. An unexpected day, regardless of whether it was the best moment or not, death ripped from her side the woman who had accompanied her since before she was born, who held the other end of the umbilical cord that transmitted life to her existence. Tati really felt alone. She would continue to live without her mother at her side, although she would not know how, but that was what the Supreme Being had imposed on her. Her brothers were still present, day after day they gave her the great support she needed. That strengthened her every moment. She really needed that support to resist the hostilities that life presented to her.

There were never missing admirers with proposals for her and her young son. Proposals that, although they seemed sincere and interesting, did not stop her aspiration. She knew what she wanted. Her studies still were her main purpose. She loved studying, there were no excuses for no continuing. People coined endless excuses not to try and achieve study goals, because they are just cheap excuses for those who do not have enough courage to perform, she thought.

Among the suitors, Tati met a handsome and decent gentleman, who in the nearer future would become her husband, the companion of her life. This must have been written in some page of the book of life. He would become the heart dad for her son and the exemplary father for those who were still to come.

His behavior did true honor to his name. That man with a tender, shy look and brown eyes that reflected the transparency of a big heart, of enormous inner beauty served her unconditional love in a silver platter. The pure feeling was so relevant that it relegated to the background any known notions of physical beauty. This was a simple complement to his inner qualities.

Tati married her new love in the mid—eighties, but not before making sure that her purpose of obtaining an academic degree would be respected. Several times she had to stop, but she would never abandon her dreams.

The former black girl was once again married. Her partner, her other half, was a man considered white by the society in which both lived. As fruits of this union, the desired children arrived. Each one of them arrived at the appropriate moment, filling the space that life had reserved for them, thus completing the exact family, consolidating the fullness and true love that strengthen a lasting home. There were five reasons for her life: her husband, whom she loved, and each of her offspring, who occupied a sacred place in her heart.

The former black girl, who never feared challenges, felt much stronger to continue. She was accompanied, very well accompanied. Now she had the support for every one of her decisions. Her ideal companion, the one who was present at each moment, who knew how to fill the emotional void left by her mother when she passed away. He brought a tea, a warm broth, or a pain reliever to her bed, whenever necessary.

At other times, he provided the support and advice of that father who was absent during her childhood. He also knew how to combine with all this the love of passion that complements a life.

However, there were not missing moments when introducing her husband to a colleague at work or at college, listened to the following:

—Damn, and how did you get up that blonde man?

—Just a moment, change the question please. Why do not you ask him how he did to get this beautiful lady?

—It's true, I had to wait a lot, and beg her to accept me.

—But how to understand my people! It is impossible to assimilate such imprudence and disrespect —he replied.

Whenever it happened, the person in question left a trail of silence in the air, or changed the subject by looking down.

—Oh, what a world this is. What a pity that a woman has such a petty thought.

In truth it is a pity that such a sublime being, as a lady, is underestimated in such a way. I can never understand, that after this man waited for two years for an acceptance of mine, another woman asked me such a stupid question. Is this fair? Holy racism! And the good thing is that sometimes this is precisely a person that projects the living expression of a skin with a high concentration of melanin. Where is the self—esteem? Oh, God, where is it? —Tati told herself.

Those and many other expressions that happened in the daily life of the former black girl evolved in her thoughts until she began to reflect on it.

Chapter XVII

—Hello, Maly!

—Hello, Tati, how are you?

—It is an honor to receive you in this your home after so long. Tell me, Maly, how is that life there, in New York, in the big refrigerator.

—Nothing especial, just working to pay the bills.

—Ah, ha, ha, ha, so it is what people living there say. But they like to live in the Big Apple.

—You know, Maly, one gets used to it.

—Come, let's go to the terrace, so long ago that we did not have a coffee and we evoked the old times. I hope this time you stay with us for a few days.

—Well, although I have several things to solve, I could not come for a long time. I will only stay a week in this city.

—I already imagined it, you are always in a hurry, living as if you still had babies, ha, ha, ha. I wonder when you will come for a couple of months to enjoy your land.

—You´re right, Tati. But we must pay the rent month by month, and if I miss the job I do not get money to pay. Then the landlord would take me to court and kick me out me out of the apartment.

—I know, it is hard. Tell me, what about your husband?

—He's back late today, he has a ship owners' summit.

—A wine first, Maly? —Tati asks her.

—What brand do you prefer? So that Nina can serve it.

—You know my favorite one.

—You're still faithful to the same wine, you don't get lost.

—Tell me something about Carlita. I haven't heard from her for a long time.

—She is enclosed in the Bronx. She comes little here, always busy with her new lifestyle.

—Once I find out she came to this country, but I don't even see her.

—And what's new in your life, Tati?

—You know, Maly, speaking of everything like crazy, I feel the need to write a book.

—A book? About what?

—I will put a title, "Oh, what a world is this!" I would write it with signs of exclamation, to highlight the concept.

—It sounds funny. And what is the book about?

—Uh, it would deal with many meaningless things to those situations we live under. For example, I wonder how humanity has lived so wrong, despite the years.

—How come?

—I usually wonder if the adjectives White and Black can define the color, the essence of a human being. I have not commented on these things, even with you that you have been like a sister. I have had several questions without finding answers and, somehow, I would like to share with the rest of the world.

—I should conclude that the concept related to white or black is rather based on a latent feeling that generates a kind of behavior, a result of the experiences of every human being. I think that these elements are responsible for the formation of each individual, and end up creating a person with soul, heart, feelings and white behaviors, or, on the contrary, a person with soul, heart, feelings and black behaviors.

—Uh, I don't understand you very well, but explain me a little more.

—Let's see how I explain it. Let's say that according to the definitions of the words black and white, it is not appropriate to apply them to qualify the color of a skin. I think that these adjectives do not really qualify to use them as an identity of ethnicities, groups, much less of races. For no race turns out to be completely good or completely bad. I have analyzed the terms in question, believe me. I have meditated a lot about them, and I always conclude understanding that... White. According to academic definition, it is the most protective color of all, brings peace, comfort, alleviates the feeling of despair and emotional shock; it helps to cleanse and clarify emotions, thoughts and spirit. It is the color that can make you feel freedom and forget about the oppressions.

—Oops! Sorry, all the black slaves must have felt the full weight of slavery in the presence of the white slave master.

—Well. Now I'm understanding you, Tati, and I think it does make sense.

—I would like someone to tell me why I did not perceive this sense of peace, protection, relief, etc., when at my side was a white person, stalking me for being black, black in quotes when skin color is concerned, because the meaning of that word does not adjust to the inner reality of the individual.

—How come?

—It is quite contradictory to understand. If we could ask those blacks of the sinister times of slavery why they felt horror, tachycardia, despair, bitterness, fear, when they saw the imposing figure of the white master approaching them.

—How come?

—We could not resemble the sensations described in the definition of the word white, which generated the presence of the white executioner to the poor and unfortunate being black, submitted by Whites to the odyssey of slavery. You remember that according to the history white masters sentenced the Negro for the simplest reason, to receive, say, fifty lashes on their bare skin for the sole purpose of imposing a meaningless rule. They were supposed to understand that another man was their owner, and therefore, he had the right to deprive them of their freedoms and use them as best he liked.

—How hard was that, huh?

—Yes, it was. Do you think that a slave could have understood that the white man was his owner and had the right to abuse him that way? It is necessary that someone explains to us how we could qualify a beautiful, pretty, gorgeous, white creature, of resplendent blue, green, amber, tender eyes. A creature that in the annals of the History of mankind has been able to subdue his or her fellows to the indescribable chain of torture we have known through the historian's pen. I'm sorry, but I find it very hard to justify — said Tati.

—Oh, just remember those immensely inhumane dealings to which they were subjected? — said Tati—. The master cut the slave a toe, for the sole purpose of ensuring that those men could not run or walk away and escape the mistreatment to which they were subjected. Tied them to a tree trunk and whip them a hundred times. The Masters beat the slave to the last sigh, in front of the relatives to serve as a lesson to any of them who tried to free themselves from slavery to which they were subjected.

—To be fair, those who mistreated the hapless Negro all the time were the white masters —said Maly.

—Beware, slavery has not been applied only to those of black color as we have seen in the beginnings of history. Remember that we have read about all these horrors in the pages written by our historians. Even in the Bible writers tell us about it.

—It's true. Your reflections have left me astonished. It seems that we read all that just to meet the school qualifications, but in truth one does not stop to analyze it. Perhaps it is so inexplicable that we read that unconsciously our mind rejects it instead of assimilate and analyze it. Even when we see it in the cinema, we resort to a defense mechanism and assume it as a fiction, rather than a reality.

—Oh, do you think that American emancipation has a slight raison d'être? No, Maly, nooo. That was just a make believe to hide the abuse of the slaves. In truth there would be no human form to compensate the rate of cruelty lived since then, which in fact has left its perpetual mark.

—Do you remember that the white masters were the owners of the Negro? In quotation marks, of course, because the use of these terms don't adjust to their true meanings.

—We have yet to ask, Maly, why that man considered himself superior, could not understand that he was before another human being like him, only with a skin pigmentation different from his. How obscure the understandings and feelings of the white could have been as a rational creature that did not harbor the ability to recognize another being of the same species, only because of the color of the skin, or his feelings were so dark, and his feelings only cast pure darkness, wickedness and horror.

—Understanding the statement that we are what we have inside, we would have to conclude that the true color of the human being comes from the inside. And it is worst if we mention the part in which those same people were subjected to being stamped on their skin with ignited irons as well as cattle and horses, which even for them is a cruel act. I imagine what affected those men subjected for the sole purpose of being identified by their white masters as cattle of

133

their property. God, what a horror! They were so insensitive! Even when the moans of their victims overpassed infinity, were not enough to touch the fibers of a white soul? Could there have existed a white reasoning that would honor the color of their skin? Had the tortured animals' legs instead of human legs, or hooves instead of fingers, contrary to the masters?

—It is true, Tati, refreshing the memory the white men also used them to satisfy certain sexual pleasures that were unable to reach among them.

—Maly, the history will always be one, although it has been written from different angles and with different pens.

—Let's suppose that today some of those black slaves of the white master lived and we asked him if he felt peace, tranquility, protection, security, and harmony. When he saw the illustrious figure of his white executioner approach, would he answer yes? I don't think so. The individual is what he projects.

—In order to visualize a possible answer to so many questions, I infer that white or black should not and should never be applied to describe the pigmentation of the skin. That these terms generate a total dissociation of their essences.

—However, after a thorough review of the meaning of the word black, we have the following definition: Black, describes the color totally dark as charcoal, and in fact lacking in all color, mysterious, is associated with infinite silence.

—It would be favorable to analyze a bit that definition of the Royal Academy. Since you are understanding, my friend, I would like you to remind me of some of the mistakes that those black men made.

—Well, I understand that the deadly sin they committed was to try to escape such harsh mistreatment of those who were victims, including women and children of their own ethnicity. Women who in addition to being tortured were also used to satisfy the sexual urges of the Masters, who also made persecute the one who was full of courage and tried to escape. Everything in order to return him to his properties, they lashed him to death to make him die in front of the other slaves. So they gave a collective lesson to other who intended to do the same.

—If we put everything in its place, we would have to ask who the true Negro was in those times, and even today. Understanding that the subjected man was obliged to carry out the work of the agricultural field from sun to sun, without the right to rest, complaints or remuneration. Only with the view that I bought him, so he's my property.

Thus they were obliged to carry the products like oxen, to plow the land and countless strong works with those who condemned even to those who were to be born. Since they fell into their mother's womb they were sentenced, for they were born slaves and had no right to be educated or to study as the children of the masters. Quoting those facts as things from the very remote past, without looking to remove old wounds, we can review the story more recent.

—Oh, Tati, I really feel a little dazed. Wow, I think it is a good idea to make a book about it.

—Thanks. But wait, if we fly back a little in time, we fall at the time of the Führer, the defender of the Aryan race, considered by him as the superior race for the color of the skin and the unique aspects of physical traits. Adolf Hitler, in his fury to keep pure his race, devastated half humanity, torturing and killing anyone who considered that he was not up to his race. He wanted to clean the world, according to his judgement. That is, to build a world in his image and likeness, apparently. Hitler starred in the Holocaust, an event recorded with blood ink. As the story tells it was the great feat of a cruel leader. It was the product of a darker sentiment, where an average of eleven million people, among whom more than six million were Jews, and at least one million of the executed were children.

—What a terrible tragedy, Tati!

—The great whites also founded his horrendous feats in useless reasons, such as political ideals, religion, and homosexuality. Facts like those were recorded between the years 1941—1945 of our civilized era. Were Hitler and his comrades really white? A white image would convey the sensations of horror, agony, and despair, which without a doubt provoked the possible presence of whoever of these characters cited above?

—Answer it yourself, my dear. Just imagining the terrified looks of these victims might be enough to answer if the black and white definitions would be in line with the aforementioned actions.

—Who is the true Negro —I wonder. There are endless recent events that would fill thousands of pages of a book, I think. A whole world dismayed, awakening a new day, in a sunrise to see and hear a news in development transmitted by all existing media.

—It was the heartbreaking news and depressing images of the horrific massacre of twenty boys and girls, plus six adults in a school in Connecticut, the United States. Obviously, black had to be the subject, for his acts thus consecrated him. Do the illustrious Knights of the Ku Klux Klan and those who perpetrated the human losses of the terrified September 11 have a white image?

—We should go back to the time of Creation.

—Of course... According to the Holy Scriptures, Lucifer was considered the most beautiful angel to dwell in the heavenly mansions, but he was tempted by the unworthy feeling of vanity and envy. This led him to feel superior and to confront and challenge his creator. Such was the magnitude of his disobedience, it resulted in the expulsion of the celestial courts. Since then he dwells in the dark depths of the earth, and is considered the most horrific of evil spirits, identified with blackness and darkness, regardless of the physical qualities that distinguished him among others when his conduct was correct.

From a clear perspective, it is well understood, that the feelings and behaviors that each individual develops, puts him in his true identity with respect to the color that radiates from deep inside. His acting makes him white or black. We can all be white if we adopt the behaviors according to the Biblical commandments.

It has always caused me laughter and sadness, when one of my children says that being black is a pain. Every time he expresses his theory, he ends up saying "Thank God I'm White".

—Oh, does he say that?
—You know that if we analyze his expression, as to the skin's qualifiers, we would have to give agree with him; because more than a condition could be considered a serious pathology, there are many who die for that reason, regardless of their standing tone.

Saying that individual is black is equal to say that individual does not serve, is a monster, a public danger, etc. Therefore it is not possible to generalize people by ethnicity. These respond to personal qualities of skin color and physical traits, etc., and should not be used to label, I think these customs merit a thorough review.

—You're right.
—I wanted to outline some facts known to the great majorities, with the sole purpose of

sustaining clearly why the day came when I understood that my requests for God to make me white were vain.

—How come, Tati?

—Oh, my friend, could you tell me what the skin is and what is its function?

—Well, according to what I remember from the times when we studied in the secondary school, scientifically the function of the skin is unique and exclusively to cover the tissues of the body. This function is to be the body's largest organ.

—Perfect, Maly! The skin does not have the power to act, decide or perform any behavioral action, right? It would be impossible for a skin to grip a firearm and shoot at someone, or to topple a commercial plane laden with people full of dreams and desires to live and have nothing, absolutely nothing to do with the political—social system that live human beings, right?

—Of course not.

—So why discriminate against the color of the skin?

—In my opinion, it is the person who thinks, acts and executes any action with mind, soul, heart and feelings. Black or white feelings, regardless of the degree of pigmentation of their skin.

—Regardless of their tone —Maly reacts.

—Oh, what can tell us about these characters and the unforgettable Nelson Mandela and the non—globally recognized Mrs. Chucha, an anonymous heroine for the world, but great in her community of Dominican Republic. A humble woman who dedicated more than half her life to educate and protect helpless girls and boys, giving them a decent house to live and grow under her love and care.

—Moreover, those doctors who save lives and help alleviate the desperate pains in humans and animals. Scientists in all the branches, who share the gifted of intellectual level, even being of different races and colors —said Tati.

—The irony is that these things are done in the name of the Creator —Maly interrupts.

—God made no exception of people by colors, if they were different, only all whites or only all blacks would qualify for certain capacities.

—It would be interesting the answer we would get, if we ask any of those who had the opportunity to receive the visits of some of the characters mentioned. Tell me if the aforementioned figures inspired them peace, protection, security, serenity and relief as they approached them.

We would understand that, being their skin black, they had to radiate the opposite, as well describes the meaning of black as color. I still wonder if those who have perpetrated the great massacres of mankind should be called whites. Or if everyone who lives properly within society must be called black, only by their skin. Also peeking to the everyday actions of ordinary people, who possesses certain tones of clear skin, often they express opinions that reflect them lousy. That girl is very pretty. But she is black." For God's sake, analyze just a little bit, what they are really saying.

I, from my position as an ex—black girl, would just like to call on humanity, without generating a confrontation of races, but quite the opposite.

In every social and scientific field, it has always been contemplated to give way to the new theories, and then it turns out that they generate great changes in humanity. Philosophy has not ceased to be the mother of all sciences.

It is, therefore, that I want to offer a philosophical contribution to the contemporary and future generations. We are white or black for our behaviors and

142

actions, for our feelings and attitudes, not for the levels of concentration of melanin that determine the tones of the skin. Under that there are not two identical skin tones, we are not a lot of people with white skin and another lot of people with black skin. On the contrary, there are as many millions of skin color as millions of human beings on the Earth's surface. Neither in parents nor in children tends to repeat the same skin tone. I think that even in identical twins does not always occurs that phenomenon.

It would lack of meaning the existence of two ends based on skin color, because I do not think they exist. I have not read any scientific research that demonstrates if the same skin tone is repeatable, as well as it is determined through the fingerprints and DNA, to cite an example.

If the mentality is not changed in that sense, the controversy would remain ill–founded for centuries and centuries. It would never end the rivalry. It would be sensible to contemplate the following: If your behavior fits the definitions of white, then you are white. If on the contrary, you act according to the characteristics of the black color, you are black, regardless of the skin pigmentation tone that you had to carry by the genes inherited in the concentration of melanin, the substance that defines the color of the skin, the eyes and the hair of each one.

—Of course, Tati, now I understand the concept of ex—black girl.

—God makes us white from the embryo in the womb of the mother, Maly.

—Those labels are put by man, through insults and mockery, not God, the creator of all.

—That's right, Tati, you've managed to keep your forehead high. You have become a mother and a teacher of hundreds of girls and boys, who have come to you in different stages and with different motives. I have seen how they have been attracted by love, peace and understanding that radiates the light of your gaze. And I even wondered what they see in you, why they call you mommy, aunt or godmother, without being your kin.

—Ah, those are the reasons why I have concluded that I am what I project. What inspires me is what describes the characteristics of white color, so God made me white. And not only the children, Maly, in recent times I have been called mother by young people and teenagers who, in some way, have lacked the affection and warmth of a mother and have found them in me. I have been called aunt by those who have

144

appreciated me so much that they have wanted to feel familiar with me, moved by the appreciation, the relief, the comfort and the peace that my color provides when I am present.

—I have actually witnessed that you have had a word of encouragement when someone next to you has needed it. From a very young age, you worked in literacy work for children with limited resources. You founded the Psycho Pedagogical College nest of love for a remote community, in the heart of a sector of scarce resources, providing the reachable support that you have. I particularly highlight this help wherever I am. And I myself am one that although I have sisters of blood, I feel that you have always filled a special place, that makes me feel like my true sister. Tati, you know I've always told you about it.

—You have also done an evangelization work in and out of the country for young children and adults. You've founded several Bible schools.

—That is for the honor and glory of God. Why do you think, Maly, that today I say thank God because you made me white, although I did not know it. Thank you because —not too late— I understood why my request was not the right one at that time. I imagine how the creator would laugh at hearing my desperate request. Today, as the former Black girl, I feel ready to make a call to all those regardless of race or physical build, or in what part of the world they are, but who have lived and are living situations similar to mine. Understanding that others are also teasing objects: fat, skinny, tall and short, very clear skin, today I invite you not to be confused by senseless mockery, the truth is unique. There can be no one ugly or beautiful, each face is unique, and each phenotype is different. Therefore, we are incomparable. We are perfect cases, full of virtues and flaws, that's all we are.

—This old and useless, inherited struggle between black and white, based on the color of the skin can never get anywhere. It really lacks logic and is baseless. You will be assured by this former black girl you have in front of you, my sister.

—It has no basis — she continued—, because just as the illustrious British philosopher John Locke argued, "The child is born a shallow table, a tabula rasa", that is filled according to the circumstances surrounding him or her. Every child is born white and is stained according to the image that projects with their feelings and attitudes. Therefore, if society fills that table of frustrations, that will result in vulnerable minds.

146

—I think parents carry on their shoulders
the main task of formation, since they are
developing in the womb of the mother.
Parents are the first forgers of each
individual's behavior, but in a very
irresponsible way they want to carry their
guilt to society. But what society, my sister, if
society consists of ourselves.

—Attention, parents, educate your
children as white children at home, which is
the real school. That way, when you deliver
them to the great society, everyone will speak
the same language. Teach your children that
we are all equal human beings. Teachers:
continue the work of parents in schools.
School authorities: make a real curriculum
change in the educational method,
incorporating a new system of education to
achieve the necessary social change that can
transform the world. This will be the day that
will gradually overcome this incessant struggle
of discrimination.

Academic and intellectual training without
a good reinforcement of morality, is like a
table with only three legs. For example, an
individual ends his long career and goes to
serve society, but his ego is so hurt that it
does not allow him to exercise his faculty a
lifetime without being assaulted by those
frustrations generated in his development. I

have always had the feeling that the reasons why so many suicide and homicides happen, come from those weak areas of the human being.

I have heard many times say that the United States brought God out of school because no religion is allowed in the classroom. I have wondered about it, is it not that the federal government welcomes the Constitution, which declares freedom of religion and directly delegates to the parents the responsibility to evangelize, according to the culture and beliefs of each family around the undisputed existence of a single God, expressed in different ideal cults of the unique Divinity?

I wonder considering that in its emblem is officially registered his undeniable existence, when we read the sentence "In God We Trust", stamped for its maximum spread in all the most popular paper bills and coins. I think that the real intent of those measures taken is to respect the right of each parent to direct and decide for their children the religion to follow, because in them, and only in them, that responsibility lies.

—It is an interesting point.

—Returning to the initial topic, Maly, the day of my death, in a journey without return, if we have not exceeded that mindset, I will try to find myself there with the illustrious white knight Martin Luther King Jr. I will smile at him and say: "Brother, keep on waiting for your dream, there is still a long way to go to abolish the terms for which you dreamed and fought. You who enjoyed the ability to see a little beyond that many.

You who have planted great thoughts that will never die, that continue to speak through your voice to those who today fight for the cause and those who are missing to come." I do not know if he can understand my broken English, but I will tell him: "We already sit in the same classrooms, but we still do not share our feelings and ideals. We still need to learn to truly love each other, with the love that God puts in our hearts, and that Jesus Christ confirmed us from the top of the cross."

—But it's a long way to reach it, because the mockery of the poorly called skin color, race, religion, hair texture and even physical texture persists.

—The mockery has never stopped. At a general level many are harassed by the ghost of bullying, as they call on your land. Some sadly fail to overcome the oppressions, fail to discover in time that everything is a farce and that the real white—black, pretty—ugly, goes far beyond what our eyes can perceive, and that does not fit in the tone of a skin, and often end up turning to the tragic exit of a suicide, how sad!

—Much has been accomplished.

—But even so contemporary education does not allow the human mind to assimilate those achievements. Today, hundreds of thousands of white women and men invest high sums of money only in order to show off the characteristic traits of a black man or a black woman. I tell you, brother that surgeons are giggling, that women are put big booties and thin waists, which are exposed to the strong tropical sun to darken their skins, and even more are subjected to strong rays in special machines to tan the skin, because they want to look darker, ah and they increase the thickness of their lips. And they're still calling the others black. Do you understand that? On the one hand they are persecuted and detested by white skinned, and on the other they want to imitate them, and they want to look like them.

—It involves a complex vision.

—They said to their children, "Do not play with blacks, that you'll be blemished." "A black person is pork food", "Come here, that the black ghost takes you in his sack"; "He

150

was wronged by him, he had to be black." Those and so many other empty expressions are nothing more than prejudices of the poorly educated and confused, so they must disappear from popular slang; It is up to the parents to do so, as long as they are not too busy with technology, politics and —why not— also with vices and drugs.

—It is a real photography, Tati

—I tell you, little sister, that one spring afternoon I was in the backyard playing stop with my children, when I said to them: "Write a name that starts with the letter **M**. Each one wrote the first one that came to his mind, and when I asked him to reveal it, one said Mary, the other read Miguel. The smallest, who was only seven years old, responded hurriedly "maldito negro", damned black. Without understanding the reason for her expression I reproached her, and she justified herself:

—You said to write a name with "M", and that was the one I wrote — while she was showing off her sheet.

—And that's a name? —I asked, receiving an affirmative answer. You can imagine how we all laughed. Then I explained that it was an insult to black skinned people. Now that lets me understand that these expressions are so natural that they are inherited as proper nouns.

Today I smile as an ex—black girl, remembering what I lived in my childhood.

Today I make mine the words of actor and activist Ossie Davis, when he read the eulogy dedicated to Malcolm X, in 1965: "Malcolm had ceased to be black years ago, it had become a word too small, too weak, and insignificant to him. Malcolm was greater than that, he had become an African—American, and desperately he wanted, that we, that all his people, became also African—Americans." Actually, who are the real blacks?

—Tati, you have left me breathless. I feel so real everything you've said, that you really leave me speechless. I don´t know what to say, I don´t know.

—And what about this other part: I have noticed that often people around me and love me use one of the degrading expressions to the color of the skin, "It had to be done by a Negro." It is way to scold a slight reproachful conduct of someone, if the person is dark skin. If he or she is clear skin the person then whispers: "That wretch seems black."

When the speaker suddenly realizes that I'm at his side, smiling tells me "Oh, sorry, you know you, it does not have to do with you." It happens a thousand times. That is something more that confirms to me that inside there is the conviction that he is black by his acts and not by the skin.

"In the beginning God created man," says in the Bible, in Genesis, the most read and accepted book in the world, right? God only created the man. Whoever determined the castes was the same man, not God. What God did, then man undid it. Therefore, one should begin to desist from racial differences, based on these theories, as the other explanations on the different shades of skin are still in search but have not been found.

Together we can make discriminatory and racist expressions become obsolete and disappear from our lexicon. Then, there will be no more parents grieving, crying the suicide of innocent children who did not manage to overcome the strong oppression of their habitat. And homicidal and suicidal adults.

This story will not have a final point until racial discrimination in the world has been overcome... The ex—Black Girl now is done and happy.

From the beginning of this narration, I have wanted to suggest that instead of battling with the bully that makes fun of you, battle with yourself to be the best you can be.

Understand that none of your equals has the power to hurt your feelings, only if you let it happen. You are not enslaved to ignorance. Lift up your face and shoulders and prove they are all wrong. Each one of you are unique, beautiful creatures of the universe that cannot be duplicated, separated, or matched with.

When an uneducated person calls you "ugly", respond by saying: "No, I am just unique. That is so true that even twins have their particularities; in other words, each one of them have their own personality and body shape, even if they look alike. Every individual has distinctive traits, remember that. Do not be provoked or misled by those who are mistaken. Certainly, your acts are neither black nor ugly. Skin is only skin, and traits are only traits.

A child needs an early boost along with a quality education: an education where the child can learn to integrate himself into a new society, an education where the contemporary use of degrading terms is refrained from future generations, an education filled with human values, where the usage of the words "black or white" based on skin color diminishes completely, and at last a society where a mother or father never tells his son to not shake another black kid's hand or else he will be stained.

The different skin tones are identified by their nature and by their pigmentation. For example, instead of naming the color "white, brown, Indian, or black", it is recommended that the appropriate terms are used for the racial and ethnic groups. Such terms are based on the concentration of melanin in the skin. Those commonly referred as "black people", are those with high concentrations of melanin in the skin, the "browns" are those with a medium concentration of melanin in the skin, and those with a low concentration are those referred as "white people".

If we educate our children with the moral values of acceptance and respect of their peers, regardless of their physical qualities, then surely the negative attitude that leads to that of a social misfit will be eliminated. Moreover, the need for gang affiliation for true social acceptance, and inhumane acts committed due to social inadaptability would drastically come to an end. It is not for nothing that each one of us are given a name at birth, and it should be used solely to identify the individual.

About the author

Altagracia Cabrera was born in the city of Santo Domingo, Dominican Republic, on February 2, 1956. She pursued various technical careers, including Marketing and Cosmetology, and worked in two of the largest institutions in her country. In addition, she graduated from O & M University, in 1993, and completed her career in Social Communications. Also, she considers herself a journalist as her main vocation.

Altagracia has always been empathetic with the poor. God, Make Me White! is her first published book, from her other unpublished books.

www.lacuheediciones.com

Made in the USA
Lexington, KY
31 October 2019